SLICES OF NIGHT

A novella in 3 parts

J.T. Ellison

Alex Kava

Erica Spindler

PRAIRIE WIND PUBLISHING
OMAHA, NEBRASKA

Prairie Wind Publishing
18149 Trailridge Road
Omaha, Nebraska 68135
www.pwindpub.com

Publisher's Note: This is a work of fiction. Names, characters, places, and incidents are a product of the author's imagination. Locales and public names are sometimes used for atmospheric purposes. Any resemblance to actual people, living or dead, or to businesses, companies, events, institutions, or locales is completely coincidental.

Interior design & formatting: Deb Carlin, Prairie Wind Publishing
Book cover design: Deb Carlin, Prairie Wind Publishing
Images for Cover: iPhotoStock

Ordering Information:
Quantity sales. Special discounts are available on quantity purchases by corporations, associations, and others. For details, contact Deb Carlin at the address above.

ISBN-13-9781539480792
ISBN-10-1539480798

Photo Credits:
Alex Kava by Deb Carlin, Prairie Wind Publishing
J.T. Ellison by Chris Blanz, Cabedge
Erica Spinder by Hoffman Miller Advertising

Printed in the United States of America
10 9 8 7 6 5 4 3 2 1

DEDICATION

To Deb Carlin.
You pulled this together, an insane, thankless task.
But you did it with grace, aplomb and good humor!
Lady, you're amazing!

Erica to J.T. and Alex:
Without you this business would be a lot more difficult ~
and a lot less fun.

Introduction by Alex Kava

July 2010 Erica Spindler, J.T. and Randy Ellison, Deb Carlin and I went out to dinner at Remy's in New York City. It wasn't the first time we had all gotten together. By now we were more than colleagues. We were friends. Sometime during dinner Deb asked Erica, J.T. and I if we'd ever consider writing something together. Of course, we said we'd love to. But as writers we spend a good deal of our time alone. We need to climb inside our minds and inside our characters. Rarely do we collaborate and when we do, it's usually to contribute a short story that we've written alone but are including in an anthology.

Thankfully Deb continued to pester us. She volunteered to be the architect, to put together and format the book. I mentioned to Erica and J.T. that it would be fun if our protagonists had to deal with the same serial killer, each in her own city. From there we started developing our killer including his MO, the weapon he used, even the victims he chose. Then we decided who had to deal with him first, second and third. And that's the order the stories were written, so that we could respond to each other.

SLICES OF NIGHT is the result. We have had an incredible experience working on this together for all of you, our readers. We hope you enjoy reading it as much as we have enjoyed writing it.

Table of Contents

SLICES OF NIGHT

A novella in 3 parts

J.T. Ellison

Alex Kava

Erica Spindler

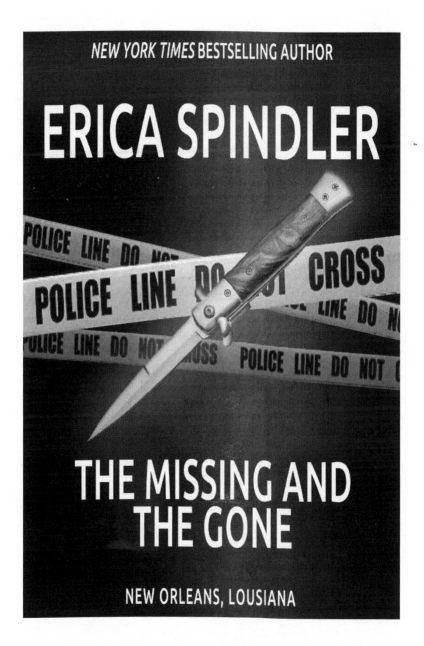

FRENCH QUARTER, NEW ORLEANS

Until today, NOPD Detective Stacy Killian figured she was made of relatively tough stuff. She'd weathered some horrendous shit, including being shot, kidnapped, and betrayed on the most elemental level. She'd figured she had seen it all when it came to pain and suffering, both hers and that of her fellow human beings.

She would never be cocky again. Never think she was so big and bad.

She'd lost the baby.

The one neither she nor Spencer had planned for. The pregnancy. Her first reaction to it had been *Hell, no. Not now, not yet.*

But then it had begun to change her. Everything from the way she viewed her body to the way she made love to her husband. She was going to be a mother. She and Spencer had made this little boy or girl with their love.

Nine weeks later, all that was gone. And she was left

3

empty, feeling lost and broken.

She wanted to weep. To wail and rage. If she allowed herself that luxury, she feared she wouldn't be able to stop. The pain, the sense of loss, went so deep, it had burrowed into her bones.

"I'm so sorry sweetheart."

The shifted her gaze to Spencer, perched at the side of her bed. She took in his strong, handsome face. Her husband. Her best friend.

Brokenhearted.

Family was everything to him. The Malone clan was as big and close knit as they came. Seven siblings, five in law enforcement, fiercely loyal to one another.

He had been so excited. So proud.

She had to be strong for him.

"I'm okay," she said. "We'll be fine."

He frowned slightly at that. "Of course we will." He took her hand, laced their fingers. "We'll have other babies."

A knot of tears formed in her throat. But she had wanted this one. It had become real for her.

"It's good we didn't tell anyone," she said. "We won't have to deal with everyone's pity."

Again, the frown. "The family needs to know. So they can help—"

"No."

"At least your sister? Jane will—"

"No," she said again, softly. "This is good. I'll get back to work, and no one will know."

French Quarter
5:15 a.m.

Stacy worked the New Orleans Eighth District. The Eighth stretched from Howard Avenue to Elysian Fields, which included party central—the French Quarter. The Quarter saw lots of drunk and disorderly, pandering and prostitution, drug offenses and thefts. Murders, too. Though they typically killed each other after they *left* the party.

Dawn broke over the spire of St. Louis Cathedral. She lifted her gaze to the spire, then moved it slowly across the landscape. The Cabildo. Jackson Square. The Pontabla. Picture-postcard-perfect.

Marred this evening by emergency vehicles and crime scene tape stretched across the Cabildo's impressive colonnade.

The Cabildo was one of the most historically significant buildings in the United States, the location of the signing of The Louisiana Purchase. Rebuilt twice. Now a museum.

Hell of a place for a murder. So not politically correct.

Apparently the perp hadn't gotten the memo.

Stacy tugged on the brim of her ball cap and glanced at her partner. "Ready Patterson?"

He yawned. "As I'll ever be."

5

They crossed to the scene officer, signed the log, then ducked under the crime tape.

Shadowed. Ten degrees cooler. Oddly removed from the twenty-first century French Quarter, coming to life behind her.

Stacy could almost believe she'd stepped back in time.

Except for the vic.

She and Patterson stopped just behind the pool of blood. This woman had not been in The Quarter to party. *Homeless,* the cardboard placard around her neck announced. *Please help.*

She wondered how many folks had walked by this spot without seeing her. Or noticed her but thought she was sleeping there, like so many of the homeless across U.S. cities did, in doorways, alleys, and parks.

She shifted her attention back to the victim. Ragged blue jeans. Battered denim jacket. Long-sleeved shirt under that. Wearing a Saints ball cap, ponytail poking out the back— same as Stacy. Frayed backpack on the walkway beside her. Zipped. Robbery hadn't been a motive.

Stacy glanced at her partner. "Wonder how she avoided our sweep?"

"Must have been hunkered down somewhere. Came out after dark."

She nodded. The NOPD routinely herded the homeless out of The Quarter, dumping them at various shelters around the city. They were particularly thorough when big conventions were in town, like the medical convention currently visiting The Big Easy.

A conventioneer had stumbled upon her. A surgeon. He had tried to help but she'd already been dead. He stood at the edge of the scene now, looking anxious.

She waved the scene officer over. "Get the doc's statement and contact information, then let him go."

The officer started off; she stopped him. "And thank him for his help."

SLICES OF NIGHT — A NOVELLA IN 3 PARTS

"You okay, Stacy?"

She looked sharply at Patterson. Good guy. Decent cop. They'd only worked together a handful of times. Stacy blew through partners pretty quickly. The lucky ones were promoted. The unluckiest of the menagerie had ended up dead.

"Why do you ask?"

"You seem off, that's all."

She worked to hide a sudden uncertainty, the urge to wrap her arms protectively over her middle.

Did something about her broadcast the news? Like a tawdry neon sign at the side of the highway?

"Just tired." She fitted on her Nitrile gloves. "It's too early for this shit."

"You got that right."

She squatted beside the victim, being careful to avoid the pool of blood. The body lay crumpled, lower body supine, upper body twisted to the right, face in profile.

Stacy shined her flashlight beam on the victim's face. "Damn, she was young."

Her partner took a spot across the body from her. "No shit. I'd be surprised if she was even twenty-one."

Stacy moved the light. "Look at her hands. How clean they are." The longer on the street, the dirtier and more rag-tag they got. "She hasn't been out here long."

"Maybe not at all?"

"Maybe," Stacy agreed. "Could've been a hustle."

"Med convention brings 'em out."

"Oh man," Stacy said. With her gloved hand, she eased the denim jacket aside. "She was knifed. Looks like one blow. Clean."

Blood had drained from the wound, soaking her lower torso. Oddly, her upper torso was wet as well, her blue shirt marred by circular stains. But not blood.

Stacy frowned. "What the hell is that?"

5:42 a.m.

"Breast milk," Coroner's investigator Ray Hollister said, a short time later. "She was lactating."

Stacy stared at him, feeling his words like a punch to her gut.

"Not pregnant," he went on. "A new mother. Breastfeeding, judging by the amount of fluid."

"How new a mother?" she asked.

"I'll know after the post. There's a schedule of healing that occurs by the sixth week after delivery. The perineum, the uterus. After that, it gets tougher to calculate."

Seconds passed. The silence was punctuated by the click and whir of the crime scene camera and the murmured conversation of the techs.

Stacy shook her head. "Breastfeeding, you said?"

He nodded and she moved her gaze between the two men.

"So where's the baby?"

8:55 a.m.

The Quarter never slept, and neither did the cops of the Eighth. While the techs finished processing the scene, Stacy and Patterson canvas the area. Most businesses were just opening for the day, their employees not the same ones who had been in the night before.

They'd collected names and numbers and acknowledged they'd have to revisit most of them again later.

As the minutes had passed, Stacy's thoughts kept returning to one: Where was the baby?

"Fill me in."

Major Henry was a fireplug of a man. No neck, huge chest, all torso. He bench-pressed 450. Which was no shit— Stacy had seen him do it.

"Vic's one Jillian Ricks. Eighteen. Barely, according to the Sacred Heart Academy I.D. she had on her. Stab wound to the chest," Stacy continued. "Pierced the lung and heart. Surgical precision. Conventioneer found her around 3:00 a.m."

"He checks out," Patterson offered. "He had just broken away from a group to go to his hotel."

"No other identification than the school I.D.?"

Patterson shook his head. "Ran her name through the system. No driver's license, nothing."

"Motive?"

"Not a robbery," Patterson said. "Her backpack was with her, untouched. Evening's collection in a zip bag inside. Thrill-kill, maybe. Random act." He glanced at her. "Child abduction."

Stacy leaned forward acutely aware of minutes ticking past. "There may be a child involved. An infant." Henry's expression darkened and she quickly explained.

"What other proof do you have?" Henry asked.

"None yet. Hollister promised to move her to the front of the line."

Her superior moved his gaze between them. "What are you thinking? That she was killed for her baby?"

Stacy pursed her lips a moment. "Maybe. But I don't think she had the infant with her. Last night was cold and damp. My theory is she left it someplace safe."

"With a relative? A friend?"

"Again, maybe, though people in her position usually don't have anyone to turn to. If they did, they wouldn't be on the streets."

"Theory based on what? Having a kid brings in the sympathy cash."

"No diapers or wipes in the backpack. No change of clothes, nothing. A new mother doesn't leave home without her supplies."

"How do you know so much about this, Detective? You and Malone have a kid you haven't told us about?"

She flushed. "My sister Jane. She has two."

"Have you considered she'd given the baby up for adoption? Or abandoned it? Breast milk doesn't dry up overnight."

He was right about that, but Stacy's gut was telling her Jillian Ricks hadn't abandoned her baby. She told him so. "Why so certain?"

"Hunch. Instinct." Her hands trembled, so she pressed them against her thighs. "An infant can go around forty-eight hours without nourishment," she said. "The younger the child, the more tenuous the situation. I don't know how long we have. Thirty hours? Thirty-five?" She leaned forward. "We've got to find that baby."

Henry frowned. "We're looking for a murderer, Detective. Not a baby. A theoretical one at that."

"I understand that, Major, but—"

"No buts. You find the perp, got that? That's your focus."

"Yes, sir."

"Good." He glowered at them. "So, go do it."

Sacred Heart Academy was one of New Orleans' storied institutions. An all-girls school grades K–12, with a list of society luminary graduates that would make even the most prestigious east coast school proud.

Located on St. Charles Avenue, surrounded by an iron fence, its grounds dotted by magnificent, moss-draped live oaks, Stacy had always driven by and wondered what would it have been like to attend school here. Would it be as storybook perfect as it looked?

Apparently not—Jillian Ricks had attended the academy.

More like an American horror story.

The headmistress met them at the front entrance, led them to her office.

"Have a seat." She motioned them toward the two chairs in front of her massive wooden desk. There was nothing institutional about it. With its scrolls and carvings, the desk shouted valuable antique.

"Sister," Patterson said, "thank you for seeing us."

"You said you were here about Jillian Ricks?"

Stacy stepped in. "That's right. We understand she was recently a student here."

"For longer than that, Detectives. She attended Sacred

Heart from the first grade."

"She graduated?"

"No. Her parents withdrew her in her junior year. Right before the Christmas break."

Because she was pregnant, Stacy guessed. Though if the headmistress knew that, she doubted she would tell her. She asked anyway. "Do you know why?"

"I'm sorry, you'd have to speak with her parents about that. We were sorry to lose Rachel."

"Rachel?"

"Jillian was her middle name. She preferred it."

"We'll need her parents' contact information."

"May I ask what this is about?"

"Homicide investigation," Stacy answered. "You'll have to speak to her parents about it."

10:30 a.m.

Uptown, holier-than-thou-hypocrites. When their daughter had refused to give her baby up for adoption, the Ricks had kicked her out of the house.

Stacy didn't bother to hide her dislike. "You're telling us you put your daughter and her infant out on the street?"

"We figured she'd be back in a matter of days."

"Days? Really?"

"She had nowhere to go. We let family know they were absolutely not allowed to help her. Same for her friends' families."

Stacy had trouble controlling the anger that rose up in her. She felt the same emanating from Patterson.

They hadn't even asked why they were here.

Almost as if they'd expected it.

"And how long has she been gone?"

For the first time, Stacy saw indecision cross their features. "Six weeks," he answered.

"Not days, then." Sarcasm dripped from the words. "Have you tried to find her?"

"No. We didn't raise our daughter to be a whore. She knows what she has to do to come home."

"She'll be home any day," the mother said, looking at her

14

husband as if for confirmation.

Stacy bit back what she wanted to say. "When did she deliver?"

"The baby was a week old when she left."

"You mean, when you kicked her and her newborn out of the house and into the street."

"Our home, our rules." Mr. Ricks swept his gaze over her. "You're not a parent, are you, Detective? You'll see, a firm hand's needed. Tough love."

As if Patterson knew she was about to lose it, he stepped in. "What about the baby's father?"

"Trash."

"In your opinion," Stacy said.

"In everyone's."

"Was he still a part of your daughter's life?"

"No. We saw to that."

"How so, Mr. Ricks?" Stacy asked.

"With all due respect, it's none of your business. This is a family matter."

"It's a police matter now."

The mother spoke up. "What kind of trouble has she gotten herself into now?"

"She's dead, Mrs. Ricks," Stacy said, unable to hold back her contempt. "She got herself murdered."

11:15 a.m.

Ten minutes later, they were buckled into Stacy's SUV. She started it, but didn't shift out of park. "I hope they did it," Stacy muttered. "It'd make my day to see them cuffed and hauled off."

"No joke. They hardly flinched at the news." He held up the photo they'd supplied of their daughter. They hadn't even had one of the baby. "You need a license to drive, but any psychopath can be a parent. No questions asked." He looked at her. "They were weird about the boyfriend. Think they killed him, too?"

Before she could respond, her cell phone sounded. "Killian," she answered.

"Detective, Ray Hollister. Autopsy's complete. You want the highlights?"

"Always. Patterson's with me. I'm putting you on speaker." Stacy clicked over and set the phone on the console. "Okay, go."

"Except for the knife wound, which killed her, she was a healthy young woman. The blade entered under the breastbone and hit both lung and heart, very neat, no torn edges, in and out."

"Type of blade?" Patterson asked.

"Stiletto-type, double-edge. Five or six inches long. Frontal attack."

Stacy stepped in. "We I.D.'ed her, spoke with her parents. They claim she gave birth seven weeks ago."

"Jibes with my findings. It's in the report."

"Any sign of drug or alcohol abuse?" Patterson asked.

"None. But Tox will give us the full story."

Stacy made a sound of impatience. "What about T.O.D.?"

"Eleven p.m. Friday. Give or take."

It was 11:00 a.m. now.

Twelve hours since the murder.

"When was the last time she breastfed?"

Hollister let out a bark of laughter. "I'm good, Detective, but not that good."

"Bullshit. An estimate."

"I'm not going to pull a number out of a hat, Detective Killian, no matter how bad you want one. I can say, however, her breasts were engorged, so it'd been a number of hours, but how many—"

"Thank you. That's what I was looking for."

Approximately sixteen hours since the baby had been fed.

Thirty-two hours remaining.

"Want the report sent over?"

"Absolutely."

Patterson looked at her, frowning. "What was that about?"

"What?"

"That sound you made at my question about drugs."

"That information's inconsequential to this case. Ricks wasn't an addict."

He frowned. "How the hell do you know?"

"No need to get testy. C'mon, really, what does that have to do with this case?"

"The one we're working? A murder investigation? C'mon, Stacy, if she was involved with drugs, it could've gotten her killed. It happens every day."

He was right. It did happen every day. It could have gotten Jillian Ricks killed.

But it was wrong. Here, it didn't work.

She told him so.

He paused. The silence stretched uncomfortably between them. "What case are you working, Stacy? I'm getting the feeling it's not the same one I am."

NOON

The boyfriend, one Blake Cantor, was a chef's assistant at a local chain restaurant, Zea's. Good food. Rotisserie meats and corn grits to die for. Stacy's stomach rumbled loud enough to make Patterson chuckle.

On paper, the young man Ricks' parents had called "trash" seemed like a pretty decent guy. Full-time job, no record, clean-cut.

Paper didn't always tell the tale; she'd met some pretty amoral bastards who looked like saints on paper. People like the Ricks family.

"What's up?" Cantor asked warily. "My boss said you needed to talk to me."

"Detective Killian," Stacy said, holding up her shield. "My partner, Detective Patterson."

"We need to ask you a few questions about Jillian Ricks."

Fear raced into his eyes. "I haven't seen her for months."

"You seem a little nervous, Blake. What's wrong?"

"Nothing. I'm done with her, that's all."

"Done with her? Wow, that sounds cold."

He flushed and backtracked. "Look, I liked Jillian. A lot. But I don't want any trouble."

"Sit down, Blake."

"Why?"

He looked panicked now.

"Sit", she repeated. "Now."

He did, though he looked for all the world like he wanted to bolt. Or puke.

"When's the last time you saw her?"

"January 5th."

"You seem pretty certain about that date."

"I am. It's the day I broke up with her."

"You broke up with her? Why?"

He stared at them. "For real?"

"Why wouldn't we be 'for real,' Blake?"

"Her parents didn't send you?"

"Why would they have sent us?"

The kid looked from her to Patterson and back, as if trying to decide if they were being honest. After a moment, he sighed. "They hated me. They told me if I saw her again, they'd make my life hell."

Stacy made a sound of disbelief. "And that's all it took? You bolted like a scared rabbit?"

He flushed. "They sent a couple of guys. Beat me up pretty bad. Told me the next time I might be dead. Or worse."

"You didn't report it to the police?"

"Seriously?"

The powerful and the powerless. The dynamic that spawned many of society's ills. "She was pregnant. Did you know that?"

The blood drained from his face. "What?"

"Pregnant," Stacy repeated. "She delivered in August."

He stared at them a moment, expression anguished, then dropped his head into his hands and wept.

A knot of emotion formed in Stacy's throat. She'd been on the receiving end of some pretty slick lies; she would bet her badge Cantor's reaction was legit.

After several moments, he straightened, wiped his eyes. "I'm a dad?"

20

"It seems true."

"Is it a boy or a girl?"

Stacy realized they hadn't even asked. "I'm sorry, Blake, I don't know."

He suddenly looked confused. "Why are you here?"

"Where were you last night?" she asked instead. "Between nine and midnight?"

"Here. Working."

"You can prove that?"

"Yeah. I was on the line all night. Didn't get out of here until midnight. Had a drink with the crew after."

No help here.

Another hour gone.

"Thank you, Mr. Cantor." She stood, Patterson with her. "We'll be in touch."

"Wait!" He scrambled to his feet. The panic was back. "Why'd you want to know that? Where's Jillian?"

"Jillian was murdered last night. I'm sorry."

1:05 p.m.

"Son of a bitch, that was messed up." Patterson jammed his hands into his pockets. "Poor guy."

Stacy didn't comment. She couldn't shake the image of the young man crumbling at the news. Literally falling apart before their eyes. They hadn't been able to help him. He'd begged to know where his baby was. Again, all they'd been able to offer him was nothing.

The need to cry rose up in her throat, strangling her.

Jillian Ricks' baby was out there. Somewhere. She had to find it.

Time was running out.

"Where now?" Patterson asked.

She shifted the SUV into Drive, and pulled out of her parking spot, tires squealing.

He was looking at her strangely. She blinked furiously, cursing the weakness.

"It's okay to cry," he said softly.

"Fuck off, Patterson. I'm not crying."

"Okay then." He lifted his hands as if to ward off an attack. "My bad."

"We need a plan."

"Absolutely."

"Don't patronize me."

"Never."

9:00 p.m.

The plan had included a recanvassing of the neighborhood around the scene. The good news: a few folks thought they recognized Ricks. The bad news: no one had seen or heard anything the night before.

It'd also included reviewing the debris collected at the scene. There'd been plenty of it—it was The Quarter, after all. Cigarette butts, wrappers, gum, several to-go cups, a Cafe du Monde cup. Lots of other goodies.

Stacy had added in a trip to the morgue. To study the remains. The wound.

In the hopes the dead would speak to her.

Instead, she had ended up talking to the vic. Begging for answers. For assurance. And promising she wouldn't let her down.

"Hey, Beautiful."

She looked up to see her husband, standing in the doorway to her cubicle. Dark hair and eyes, quick smile, crooked nose. Her heart did a funny, little flip. Still, after all this time together.

"Spencer."

The tiniest wobble in her voice. Concern raced into his eyes, and she knew he had heard it, too.

"Stop it," she said.

"What?"

"Worrying."

"Sorry, babe. Goes with the vows." He lifted a white take-out bag. "I brought food." He shook the bag. "Your favorite: half-n-half po'boy, dressed."

Half fried shrimp, half fried oyster, lettuce, tomato and mayo on French bread.

The last thing on her mind was food. Something else that would cause him to worry. She forced a smile. "Abita root beer?"

"You know it."

She stood and they headed to the break room. They had the place to themselves and sat facing each other over the battered table.

He immediately dug into his sandwich. "Talk to me," he said, around a huge bite.

She forced nonchalance into her tone. "Not much to talk about. Working a new case."

She hadn't fooled him; his gaze sharpened. "Heard about it. Any leads?"

"Nothing." She unwrapped the po'boy. The seafood spilled out the sides. She popped a shrimp into her mouth, then followed it with an oyster.

"You need sleep."

"Not yet. I can't." She lowered her gaze to her food, then looked back up at him without taking a bite.

"I'm heading down to the Cafe du Monde tonight. There was an empty cup near the body. Hot chocolate."

"What's this about the vic having a baby with her?"

He had said it casually. Too casually. "Not with her. But somewhere."

"Yeah?" He chewed, expression thoughtful. "Why so certain?"

"Who've you talked to?" she asked, cheeks heating. "Patterson? Major Henry? They tell you to come talk to me?"

He frowned. "A murder happens in the Eighth, I know about it. And nobody tells me to 'talk' to you, Stacy. You're my wife." He paused. "What's going on?"

"I'm sorry." She reached across the table and caught his hand, curling her fingers around his, thankful for his strength. "I'm on edge about this case."

"Tell me about it. Maybe I can help."

She began, laying it out the way she saw it. A young vic. New mother. Breastfeeding. The reasons why she believed that the night she had been killed, Ricks had left her baby behind. She shared how the hours since the murder seemed to be clicking off in her head.

"What about who murdered her? Who've you talked to?"

"Ex-boyfriend, the baby's father. Her parents. Both have alibis. We're looking for others."

Stacy took a swallow of the root beer. "It's someone we haven't interviewed yet. Friend or acquaintance. A stranger. Could've been a thrill kill. A gang initiation. Someone who has issues with the homeless." She paused. "Or, someone who wanted her baby."

Stacy glanced down at her sandwich, realizing she'd only picked at it. She carefully folded the paper wrapper back around it. She lifted her gaze to her husband's. "Here's the thing, this wasn't some hack-and-slash. This perp attacked her with surgical precision."

She took another swallow of the soft drink, using the moment to collect her thoughts. "He knifed her head-on. Left side. The angle of the wound tells us he's right-handed. He came in low, slipped the blade in. No struggle. Took her completely by surprise."

"She was walking toward him," he said.

"Yes. Keeping to the shadows. The fringes." She lifted the root beer bottle, then set it down without drinking. "Nobody begs on that corner. St. Peter and Chartres? No way. Too close to the Square. Too much NOPD presence."

"She was heading where? What direction?"

25

"The River." Home. To her baby. "That's all we have."

"Cafe du Monde, what are your objectives?"

"See if anybody recognizes her. Find out if she was there last night. And if she was, did she have a baby with her."

"Then what?"

"If she didn't, I'll know I'm right. She left the baby someplace for safekeeping."

"With someone," he said.

"No. She had no one."

"Of course she did," he said reassuringly. "What kind of mom leaves an infant alone?"

"She didn't have anyone, Spencer. She was afraid."

"You have me, Stacy."

"What does—" She searched his gaze, suddenly realizing what he meant. "This isn't about me."

"Come on, sweetheart. Don't you think it's possible your in-stints are scrambled right now?"

"They're not."

"That they could be driven by the miscarriage?"

Angry, she jerked her hand away. "They're not."

"You know nothing about this girl," he said softly. "Not what kind of mother she was. Not—"

"I know this."

He made a sound of frustration. "Sweetheart, this isn't about our baby."

Her mouth went dry. "I can't believe you would say that to me."

"It makes sense. Stacy, honey, we lost our baby, there was nothing you, or I, could do." He paused. "And now you're trying to save hers."

"No." She shook her head. "This young woman was a mother. She left her baby behind, somewhere safe. It was a cold, damp night. Then she was murdered. Her baby is alone and—" Angry tears choked her. "Wow, I married a detective and psychoanalyst."

"I know you, Stacy. Better than anyone."

"I used to think that."

She started to stand, he stopped her. "You didn't cry."

"What?"

"When we lost the baby."

"You keeping score, Malone?"

"We wanted that baby. Losing it broke my heart. Didn't it break yours?"

She couldn't breathe. "Stop this."

"Didn't it?"

"Yes," she whispered. "It did. Are you happy now?"

He stood and came around the table, drew her into his arms. She resisted a second, wanting to hold onto her anger, the strength it gave her, then melted into him.

After a moment, she lifted her face to his. "I know I'm right about this, Spencer. I need you to trust me."

He rested his forehead against hers. Searched her gaze. "I believe in you, Stacy. And I'm with you, one hundred percent."

10:10 p.m.

Cafe du Monde. Perhaps the most famous eatery in New Orleans, a city known for food, and they only served three things: cafe au lait, milk, and beignets—New Orleans' powdered-sugar-dusted version of a donut. As such, Cafe du Monde stayed busy. No such thing as a lull here even though they were open twenty-four, seven.

Stacy figured Ricks wouldn't have attempted to grab a table. No, she would've waited in the take-out line. Stacy did the same, though she could've used her badge to go directly to the window. Besides not wanting to start an all-out riot, she wanted to recreate Ricks' experience, see what she'd seen.

Lots of people, tourists and locals alike. Street performers: a human statue over by the closed information center, a group of boys at the amphitheater.

She reached the front of the line and held up her shield. "Detective Killian. I need to ask you a few questions."

The girl at the window looked unimpressed.

"You work last night?"

"I work every night. 6:00 p.m. to 4:00 a.m."

"Do you recognize this woman?" She slid the photo across the counter.

The girl studied it a moment, then nodded. "Yeah, she

comes around sometimes."

"Was she here last night?

"Yeah, I think so. Always gets a hot chocolate."

The folks in line behind her were getting restless. Stacy heard a few of them grumble. She ignored them, slipped the photo back into her jacket pocket.

"She have a baby with her?"

"Not last night."

Stacy's heart quickened. "But she does sometimes."

"Yeah." Her gaze shifted over Stacy's shoulder. "You gonna order something? If not, my manager—"

Stacy cut her off. "When's the last time you saw her with her baby?"

"I don't know. A couple days ago. Before it got cold."

"Hey, lady!" the guy directly behind her said. "You mind? We're waitin' here!"

White-hot anger exploded inside her. Stacy swung around, all but shoving her badge in his face. "Back the fuck off! Police business."

The guy's eyes widened and he took an instinctive step backward. She knew if he reported the exchange she'd be dragged in front of the PID and get her hands slapped. Abuse of power. Not the profile the city wanted for its department.

Right now, she didn't give a shit.

Twenty-four hours since the murder.

Baby unaccounted for longer than that.

She swung back around. "You ever see her with anyone?"

"No. Just the baby."

Stacy narrowed her eyes. "Think hard. You ever see her talking with anyone? It's important."

The girl started to say no. Stacy saw the word form on her lips. Suddenly her gaze slid over Stacy's shoulder. In the direction of the street performer, posing on the edge of the plaza.

"The human statue?" Stacy asked.

"Yeah. That guy. Tin Man. I seen her with him sometimes."

29

10:20 p.m.

The Quarter was known for its street performers. Musicians, acrobats, mimes. Human statues. Like the Tin Man here. Blazing heat. Cold, rain, wind. There they stood. Frozen.

Stacy approached him. Painted entirely silver—skin, hair, gym shorts, winged shoes and hat. Eye whites looked disturbingly yellow in contrast. He stood on a silver platform. She looked up at him. "I need to ask you a few questions."

He didn't move a muscle. Stacy gave him props for staying in character. "About a friend of yours. Jillian Ricks." Still nothing. She held up her shield. "N.O.P.D."

He eyes shifted, took in the badge. "I'm working."

How did he manage to speak without moving any other muscle? Bizarre. "So am I, dude. You coming down? Or am I coming up?"

"Climbing down."

Instead, he leaped sideways off the platform and sprinted in the opposite direction.

"Son of a bitch!" She started after him, berating herself for not seeing that coming. "Police!" she shouted, darting through a crowd watching the boys compete with one another.

For a guy who spent his days not moving much, The Tin

Man was fast—and nimble.

But not fast enough.

She got close enough to bring him down as he rounded the corner onto Esplanade Ave. She tackled him and sent them both sprawling onto the pavement. She heard a sickening crack and saw a spray of blood. Somebody was going to need a trip to the E.R.

Too fuckin' bad.

Stacy wrenched his right arm around his back, snapped on one cuff, then did the same with the second.

"You never run, asshole," she said through gritted teeth. "But you do have the right to remain silent . . . "

11:35 p.m.

Stacy had called for a cruiser and let the officers escort the Tin Man to the Eighth. Now, she sat across the scarred up interview room table from him. Patterson stood by the door. She swept her gaze over him. Legal name Charlie Tinnin. Had a record, though nothing hardcore. Silver smeared by sweat and blood, cleaned away from the nasty gash on his chin and sidewalk burn on his right cheek. The doc who'd taken a look at both had pronounced him fit for questioning.

"Charlie," she flipping through his file, "you have a record. Surprise, surprise."

"I didn't do anything."

"Except run. Why'd you run, Charlie?"

"'Cuz I don't like cops. No offense."

She'd heard that one before. "You sure that's the reason, Charlie?" She waited. He frowned. "You sure it doesn't have something to do with Jillian Ricks?"

"What about Jillian?"

"You know her?"

"We've talked a couple times."

"Talked? That's it?"

"Yeah." He shifted uncomfortably. "Why?"

"Because she's dead."

The color drained from his face. He couldn't have faked that, but the reason for it was up for grabs.

"Dead," he repeated. "When—" He cleared his throat. "What happened?"

"Where's her baby, Charlie?"

"What?"

"Her baby. It's unaccounted for."

"I don't know what you're talking about."

"You are aware she had a baby."

He nodded. He reminded her of one of those bobble head toys. "So what?"

"The infant's missing, that's what."

Patterson cleared his throat in an attempt to redirect her. Stacy ignored him. "Why'd you run, Charlie?" she asked again.

"I told you. I swear."

"When's the last time you saw Jillian?"

"I don't know . . . a couple days ago. We didn't hang out."

"She have any other friends?"

"I don't . . . not that I know of. When did she—when did it happen?"

"I ask the questions here, not you. Where were you last night? Between eight and midnight."

"Working my spot."

"By Cafe du Monde?"

"Yeah."

"But you didn't see Jillian?"

His eyes darted nervously between her and Patterson. "I told you, I was working. She may have walked by, I don't know."

"Come on, she walked by? Friends say hello."

"It was busy. Med convention in town." When she simply stared at him, he added, "You stand up there without moving a muscle, see what you see."

He had a point. "Where did she stay?"

"I don't know."

"I think you do." And she did. She saw the uncertainty

that raced into his eyes. "Where'd she stay?"

"Last I—"

"Excuse me, Detectives?" The desk officer stuck his head in. "A moment."

Stacy stood and joined Patterson and the officer outside the interrogation room.

"We've got another victim."

Stacy sucked in a sharp breath. "Where?"

"North Rampart. Near Armstrong Park. Same M.O."

Stacy's heart stopped, then started again with a vengeance. "Another young woman with a child?"

"No. An old guy. Also homeless. Just happened."

The son of a bitch wasn't killing to acquire the infants. Thank God.

Stacy turned and started back into the interview room.

"Killian?"

Patterson. Confusion in his tone. She didn't stop or look back, simply returned to her seat across from Tinnin. "Where'd she stay?"

"What the hell, Killian? Release him. He's not our guy. We've got to go."

"Where'd she stay," she asked again, holding Tinnin's gaze. "I need that information. Now."

"Vic's still twitching," Patterson said. "Come on, perp could be close by."

She looked at her partner. "Go, then! I've got this."

"You're losing it, Killian. I'm going to have to report this to Henry."

"Do it then. Take my frickin' badge." She unclipped it and slammed it onto the table.

"A warehouse!" the kid blurted out. "Upriver from the Quarter."

Stacy was aware of her partner's shocked silence. She turned back to the kid. "You're going to take me to where Jillian stayed. Now."

12:10 a.m.

The Mississippi River snaked its way around New Orleans, hugging the French Quarter, feeding the city.

All along it, both upriver and down, warehouses dotted the levee, supporting New Orleans' port, one of the busiest in the country.

"Where?" she demanded, buckling in.

"Are you crazy?"

She realized she must seem that way to him. Wild-eyed from lack of sleep, an emotional wreck. Her off the rails behavior at the Eighth.

She glanced his way. "Not dangerous crazy."

"So you're not going to hurt me?"

"I'm not going to hurt you." He looked unconvinced, but buckled up anyway.

"The baby," she said, easing away from the curb. "What's its name?"

"Jillian called her Peanut."

Peanut. Stacy tightened her fingers on the steering wheel. *Be alive, Peanut. Be safe.*

12:25 a.m.

He led her to an abandoned warehouse just upriver from the French Market, at N. St. Peters and Elysian Fields. She pulled up and parked. Looked at him. "This is it? You're sure?"

"I just dropped her off here. I didn't go in."

"That'll do." She popped open the glove box, retrieved her spare flashlight and handed it to him.

He looked at it, then back up at her. "Do I have to?"

"Yeah. Man up, dude."

He grimaced. "I bet it smells in there."

It did. Of mold, unwashed bodies and God knew what else. Stacy moved her flashlight beam over the interior. Basic, metal walls and supports, concrete floor.

Jillian hadn't been the only one to call this warehouse home. Cardboard boxes, ratty old blankets.

Figures curled into balls under those blankets. A few huddled together, staring blankly at her.

Eight squatters died in a warehouse like this last winter. It had caught fire and burned to the ground.

She shuddered. "Police," she called. "I'm looking for a baby. Jillian Ricks' baby." She swept the beam over the huddled figures. "She called her Peanut."

Silence.

"I don't want any trouble. Just the baby. She's probably been crying."

The transient didn't trust anyone, particularly police. They lived on the fringe for a reason, none of them good. Mental illness. Abuse. PTSD. Bad, frickin' luck.

She dug a bill out of her pocket. Held it up. "I've got ten bucks for the one who takes me to her."

"Twenty."

Stacy swung in the direction the crackly voice had come. A woman. Face obscured by dirt and wild gray hair.

Stacy dug another ten out of her pocket. "Show me, and it's yours."

The woman pointed, then held out her hand.

Stacy closed her fist on the cash. "Nope. You have to take me to her."

The woman hesitated a moment, then got to her feet. She shuffled forward, waving for them to follow her.

She led them to a far corner of the building. To a grouping of cardboard boxes. She handed the woman the money and focused on the boxes.

A home. Jillian Ricks had built a home for her and her baby.

Emotion choked her. She moved closer. "Peanut," she called. "Make a sound for us, Sweetheart."

A low, deep growl answered her. Jillian hadn't left her child alone after all.

Stacy got to her knees. Directed her light into the makeshift home. A small, dirty white dog bared its teeth. She'd been bitten a couple times before, once by a Pit. A drug dealer had set him on her, and she'd been forced to take it down. She loved animals and had hated doing it. She prayed it didn't come to that tonight.

She shifted her gaze and the flashlight beam. It fell across a small bundle, partly obscured by the dog.

The bundle mewed weakly, like a kitten.

Stacy's heart jumped; she looked back at Tinnin. "She's alive! Call 9-1-1. Tell them there's an officer down."

"But, you're not—"

"It's the quickest way to get an emergency vehicle here. Do it!"

It occurred to her she might be down, once that little dog was finished with her. "It's okay," she said softly, hoping to reassure the animal. "I'm going to help Peanut."

She inched into the box, earning another growl. "Peanut needs food and water. And so do you. It's going to be okay," she said again. "I promise."

She crawled in, stopping every few inches to let the animal grow accustomed to her, the whole time continuing to talk softly. The dog watched her warily, muzzle quivering, but not baring its teeth. A good sign.

Stacy took a deep breath. "Good dog. That's right, good, good dog . . . I'm going to take Peanut now . . . that's right—"

She scooped her up. Cradled her to her chest. She was alive. Alive and the most beautiful thing she'd ever seen.

"Peanut," Stacy whispered, the wail of sirens in the background. "It's going to be okay now. Everything's going to be all right."

And then, Stacy began to cry.

One week later.

As Stacy walked into the squad room, it went silent. But only for a moment.

"Welcome back, Killian," Patterson said, standing. "Way to go."

Others followed his lead, calling out congratulations, clapping her on the back as she passed.

Yeah, she'd broken ranks—and been reprimanded for it. But she'd also trusted her gut and followed her instincts. Nobody understood—and applauded—that better than another cop. That it'd paid off was definitely something to cheer about.

Several minutes later, she sank into the chair across the desk from Patterson. "Looks like you managed to keep crime at bay without me."

He laughed, then shook his head. "A week's suspension without pay, Killian. That was stiff."

"But so worth it." Stacy sobered. "Sorry about that night. I was out of line."

"You were right. You saved that baby's life."

"But the bad guy got away."

A week had passed with no new leads. Nothing. The medical convention had packed up and left town, and Stacy couldn't help wondering if their perp had left with them. If she had been focused on catching him, if she had joined Patterson at the scene, while it was still white-hot, would the outcome have been different?

As if reading her thoughts, Patterson snorted. "Stop it, Killian. You did what you thought was right and followed your gut. Isn't that what a cop's supposed to do?"

"He's going to kill again."

"Yeah, he is. But maybe that little girl's going to grow up and cure cancer."

She stared at him a moment, then laughed. "We're going to be okay, aren't we?"

"Maybe."

She laughed again. "Fair enough, considering. You plugged everything into ViCAP?"

"Done. How's the newest member of your family?"

"Peanut, the wonder dog," she said, shaking her head. Child Protective Services had taken Jillian's baby until she could be joined with her father, but no way would Stacy allow that brave little pooch to be taken to the SPCA. "I swear, Spencer already loves that mutt more than me."

Major Henry stuck his head out his door. "Patterson, Killian, 10-21, Waldhorn and Adler Antiques on Royal." He paused, nodding slightly in her direction.

"Now, not tomorrow."

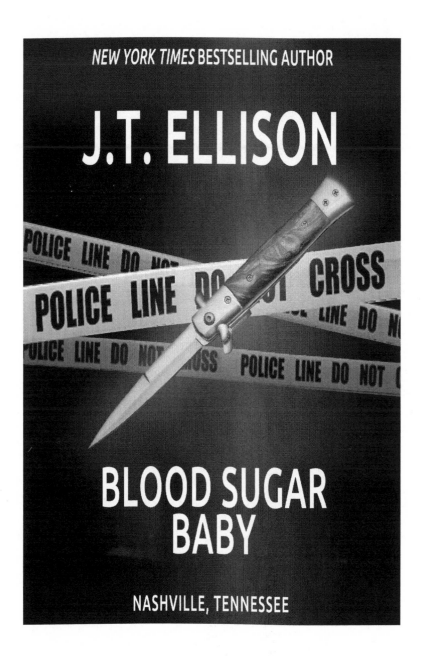

NEW YORK TIMES BESTSELLING AUTHOR

J.T. ELLISON

BLOOD SUGAR BABY

NASHVILLE, TENNESSEE

Chapter 1

Nashville, Tennessee

He was lost. His GPS didn't take roadwork into account, nor roads closed to accommodate protests; he'd been shunted off onto several side streets and was driving in circles. He finally made a right turn and pulled to the curb to get out a real map, and as he reached into the glove box— shit, he needed to get that knife out of there—he saw her. She was on the concrete sidewalk, sprawled back against the wall, a spread of multicolored blankets at her feet, staring vacantly into space. Her dirty blond hair was past limp and fell into dreadlocks, matted against her skull on the left side. He drove past slowly, watching, seeing the curve of her skull beneath the clumps of hair; the slope of her jaw; her neat little ear, surprisingly white and clean, nestled against her grimy skin. Her eyes were light. He was too far away to see if they were blue or green. Light irises, and unfocused pupils. High, perhaps, or starved, or simply beyond caring.

Perfect.

No one would miss her. And he could rid himself of this nagging fury that made him so damn antsy.

He closed the glove box and circled the block. There she sat, just waiting for him.

A sign.

A gift.

It had been a bad day. The fat ass he'd started med school with, Heath Stover, had called, wanting to get together. Stover was a classic jock gone to seed: flakily jovial, always over-the-top, clearly trying to compensate for something. JR had run into him last month in New Orleans, been forced into drinking hurricanes at Pat O'Briens, and had stupidly told Stover where he worked.

He shook his head, the scene replaying itself over and over and over. Stover bragging and braying at the top of his lungs about his hugely successful practice, his new BMW, his long-legged, big-busted bride, his offer of tenure at Tulane. The only thing off in his brilliant, wonderful life, Stover confided, was his piece on the side, who'd been pushing him to leave his wife.

In the moment, bolstered by alcohol, the camaraderie, the overwhelming need to fit in, to be accepted, to look as palatable to the real world as this fuck-up, he cast sanity aside. Arrogance overtook him, and he revealed his own career path, one that had taken him up the ladder at Bosco Blades; he was a salesman extraordinaire. No Willy Loman, though he perhaps looked and sounded a bit like the sad sack, but that was all a part of his act. He was better than that. Better than good. He was the best the company had: stock options, access to the corporate jet, the house in Aspen, all of it.

"As a matter of fact," he'd told Stover, "I'm headlining a conference in Nashville next month. Talking about the new laser-guided scalpel we've developed. Hell of a thing."

"Hell of a thing," Stover had replied. He was counting on the fact that Stover was far too drunk to recall the name of the company, and he gave him a fake number to write down, and a bogus email.

But the stupid son of a bitch had remembered the company name, had called and wormed JR's personal cell number out of his secretary, and managed to put himself on

JR's calendar. In a couple of hours, the sloth would be waiting at a restaurant several streets away for an instant re-play of their recent night in the Big Easy.

If only Stover knew what had really happened that night. About the knife, the silent scream, the ease with which the flesh accepted his blade.

He needed someplace quiet and calm to prepare himself for his night out with a "friend." He needed a drink, truth be told. Many drinks.

But the woman would do just as well. She would turn his frown upside down.

He parked a few blocks away, pulled a baseball cap low on his head, and walked back to the spot. A marble and concrete sign said he was at Legislative Plaza. The War Memorial. The Capitol rose to his right, high against the blue sky, and the small crowd of protestors with their signs held high gathered on the stairs. He needed to be careful when he passed them, not to draw their attention.

He found the perfect spot halfway down the block, shielded from the friendly mob on the stairs, and from the street, with the trident maples as cover.

And then he watched. And waited. At some point, she would have to move, and then he would follow, and strike.

To hell with Heath Stover. He had a rendezvous ahead with someone much more enticing.

Chapter 2

The homicide offices in Nashville's Criminal Justice Center had been quiet all day. It was the first Monday off daylight savings time, and even though it was barely 5:00 p.m., the skies outside Lieutenant Taylor Jackson's window were an inky black. The lights over the Jefferson Street Bridge glowed, warm and homey, and she could just see the slice of river flowing north to Kentucky. It was a moonless night; the vapor lamps' illuminations reflected against the black waters.

Her detectives were gone for the day. Paperwork had been completed; cases were being worked to her satisfaction. She'd stuck around regardless—the B-shift detectives would be here shortly, and she could hand off the department to her new sergeant, Bob Parks. He was a good match for the position and had the respect of her team, who'd worked with him for years. Parks had no illusions about moving up the ladder; he was content to be her sergeant until his twenty was up in two years and he retired. His son, Brent, was on the force now, too. Taylor suspected Parks had opted to get off the streets to give his son some room. Classy guy.

Her desk phone rang, cutting through the quiet, and she shifted in the window, suddenly filled with premonition.

"Lieutenant Jackson."

It was Marcus Wade, one of her detectives.

"Hey, Loot. We've got a problem."

"What kind of problem?"

"The kind that comes with the chief of police attached."

"I thought you went home."

"I was heading that way, but saw a cordon by Legislative Plaza where the protestors have been camped. Looked like something we might be called in on. I was right."

Taylor took a seat, opened her notebook. "What's going on?"

"They found one of the Occupy Nashville folks dead, right at the steps to the War Memorial Auditorium. Stab wound to the chest. Nice and neat, too."

Taylor groaned.

"It gets better."

"What?"

"The victim? It's Go-Go Dunham."

"Oh, son of a bitch."

"Yep. You wanna head on down here?"

"I'll be there in ten. Who all's there?"

"A shit load of protestors right now. Someone got in touch with her dad, so he's on his way. I called you first. I know you're gonna want to tell the chief."

"Oh, Marcus, you're just too kind."

"You know it," he said, and clicked off.

Normally Taylor's captain, Joan Huston, would be handling the chief, but she was out on paid leave—her first grandchild had just been born, and she'd taken some time to go be with her daughter.

Taylor hung up the phone and grabbed her leather jacket from the peg behind her door. She shrugged into the well-worn coat, retied her hair in a ponytail, grabbed her radio and set off. She took the stairs to the chief's office two at a time.

Virginia "Go-Go" Dunham was the twenty-two-year-old daughter of Joe Dunham, founder of one of the biggest healthcare companies in Nashville. His latest headline-grabbing venture was building environmentally-friendly dialysis centers, ones designed to be both pleasing to the patients and capture major tax breaks from the government. The trend had caught on—his designs had been patented and utilized to build similar centers across the country. Dunham was a pillar of the community, a regular at all the major charitable events, a contributor to the mayor's election fund, and an all-around connected guy. His one and only daughter, Virginia, known as Go-Go, had felt living up to her dad's squeaky-clean image too much trouble, and, as a difficult youngster, quickly mired herself in the social drug scene. She'd earned her moniker at fourteen, when she'd been busted dancing at the Déjà Vu strip club. This was before the new ordinance forbade touching the dancers, and, nubile, blond, busty Go-Go had taken full advantage of the situation. She was pulling down three grand a night, and putting the vast majority of that cash right back up her nose.

Several stints in rehab and a few busts later, she was supposed to have cleaned up her act. No longer a regular fixture on the nightclub scene, she'd gone back to school, earned a degree and taken a job working for her dad.

If she were still straight, how in the world had she managed to get herself dead?

Lights were on in the chief's office. This wasn't going to go over well. He was a close personal friend of the victim's father. As close and personal as anyone could be when they were involved in political endeavors together. Dunham and the mayor were fishing buddies; she knew the chief tagged along on occasion.

The offices were empty and quiet, the admin gone home for the day. Taylor was about to knock on the chief's closed door when he called out, "I hear you lurking out there, Lieutenant. Come in."

She followed his instruction.

Chief DeMike was a veteran of the force, promoted to the

head spot from within, and a welcome change from the previous incarnation, a man as corrupt as the day was long. DeMike's hair was white, his face ruddy, with cheeks and jowls that would swing in a stiff breeze. He looked a bit like an overweight Bassett hound masquerading as Santa Claus in dress blues. But he was good police, and had always been fair with her.

"You're here about the Dunham girl?"

"You already know?"

DeMike pulled a cigar out of his humidor and started playing with it. "Sugar, I know everything in this town."

Taylor raised an eyebrow.

"Sorry." He snipped off the end of the cigar, then rammed it into the corner of his mouth. He couldn't smoke it in here, not that he hadn't before, but Taylor knew it was only a comfort gesture.

"Joe's been notified. We need to head down to the scene. He's going to meet us there. He's expecting a full show, so you should be prepared."

"I am. Not a problem. But tell me, who made the call to Mr. Dunham? Seems a bit quick to me."

"Already investigating, Lieutenant? Good. I like that. He told me one of her friends called him. Apparently, she's been camping out down there with the protestors."

He stood, the bulk of his weight tossing his chair backward against the windowsill with a crash.

"I thought she'd been walking the straight and narrow of late."

"I don't know, Lieutenant. Head on down there and find out. I'll arrive with due pomp and circumstance in a few."

Taylor nodded gravely, trying not to smile. "Yes, sir."

Chapter 3

When the first siren lit up the night, he was four blocks away, at Rippy's on Broadway, sipping a Yuengling, a pulled pork sandwich smothered in sweet and tangy BBQ sauce and corn cakes with butter on order, waiting for Stover to show. The high-pitched wail made pride blossom in his chest.

It had gone gloriously. She'd never seen him coming. As he predicted, after an hour, she'd shuffled off toward the port-a-potties, and when she'd drawn near, he'd straightened his spine, let the knife slide into his hand, and stepped from the bushes. He'd become so adept at his trade that the contact he'd had with her was, on the surface, just an incidental bump. As he'd said, "Excuse me," he'd slid the knife right up under her breastbone directly into her heart. A clean cut, in and out, no twisting or sawing. Precision. Perfection.

He was half a block down the street before she hit the sidewalk.

He was so good at this. Granted, practice does make perfect, and he'd had quite a bit of practice.

He allowed himself a smile. He'd managed to salvage a very annoying day, and give himself something wonderful to think about tonight. Something to chase away the annoyance of having to play charades with Stover the fat ass tonight.

Stupid bastard. Who was more successful in their *chosen* fields?

Now, JR, stop worrying about that. Think about what you just did, how you're sitting right under their noses, having a nice little Southern dinner. Think about the edge of the blade, colored a grimy rust by the girl's blood, sitting in your pocket. Think about the way the tip fed into her flesh, and her eyes caught yours, and she knew it was you who was ending her life. These are appropriate thoughts. You can't look back to the bad things. Just stay focused on the here and now.

Stover arrived with a bellow.

JR played his part—accepting the rough handshake, making small talk, eating, drinking, pretending—all the while sustaining himself with thoughts of his light-eyed beauty, lying on the sidewalk, her heart giving one last gush of blood to her body.

After what seemed like hours, Stover called for the bill, belched loudly without covering his mouth and announced, "We need women."

The idea was repugnant to JR. Women were not for defiling one's self with, they were for the glory of the knife. Glory be. Glorious. Glory glory glorious.

Perhaps he'd had one beer too many.

But this event presented his best chance of escape. So he acquiesced, and followed Stover into the night. The street outside the restaurant was hopping, busy with tourists and revelers even on a Monday. Downtown Nashville was a twenty-four/seven world, and they slipped into the throngs without causing a second glance. Because JR fit right in. He always fit in now.

Chapter 4

Taylor arrived at the crime scene ten minutes after Marcus's call. The site was just down the street from the CJC; she could have walked it if she wasn't in too much of a hurry. But tonight she was. Containment would be key. The Occupy Nashville protestors had been causing an uproar downtown for two weeks now. Bills were being passed to stop their ability to gather freely, face-offs between the protestors and other groups had turned the mood on the steps sour, and even the people of Nashville who agreed with their agenda were beginning to turn against them.

The real beneficiaries of their protest were the homeless who spent their time hanging out in the little park on Capitol Boulevard, burrowed in between the downtown Library and Legislative Plaza. Strangely enough, the hippies and the homeless looked remarkably alike, and do-gooders answering the call of the protesters by traveling downtown to bring food and blankets didn't necessarily know the difference. The homeless weren't stupid; they took full advantage of the situation. They were being fed, clothed, and warmed daily, sharing smokes and tents with the protest-tors. Taylor didn't think that was such a bad thing, but she did wish the folks who'd rallied to the call would think to provide this kind of succor to those less fortunate on a more regular basis. If Twitter could take down a despot, surely it could help keep Nashville's homeless clothed and fed.

But that wasn't her problem right now. She needed to contain a huge local story before it got blown into a political mess.

She was an experienced detective—fourteen years on the job with Metro—so she knew better than to jump to conclusions. If Go-Go was with the protestors and had been stabbed, chances were she'd been murdered by one of her fellow demonstrators. And that news was going to go national.

As she parked, she took in the scene, one she'd been privy to too many times. Sixth Street was blockaded between Church and Charlotte, blue and white lights flashing crazily on the concrete buildings, reflecting off the black glass of the Tennessee Performing Arts Center. Thankfully TPAC didn't have anything playing tonight, the building's lobby was dark and gloomy. She could see the focus of all the attention was midway up the street, just below the steps to the Plaza.

"Lieutenant!"

Tim Davis, the head of Metro's Crime Scene unit, waved to Taylor. She waved back and headed his way, watching the crowd as she walked down Sixth. The area had been cordoned off—that's what Marcus had seen driving home— but a large crowd had gathered on either side of the crime scene. Yellow tape headed them off, but frightened eyes peered down from the Plaza, and across from TPAC a small horde of people had formed, staring curiously up the street in hopes of seeing something tawdry.

Tim was overseeing the evidence gathering. She was glad to see him on duty. Tim was meticulous, and if there was evidence to find, he'd make sure it was bagged and tagged.

"Hey, man. What's up?"

"Marcus told you it was Go-Go?"

"Yeah. Damn shame. What's the evidence telling us?"

"Single stab wound to the chest. I've been collecting everything around, but the ground's littered with crap from the protestors. Messy bunch of people." His nose wrinkled in disapproval. Tim liked things straight and clean. It's what made him so good at spotting objects that were out of place.

"We've got cameras here, don't we?"

"Yeah. I've got a call into TPAC. Their security footage will give us the best chance of seeing what happened."

"Good. Let me know if you find anything else. Is that Keri working the body?"

"Yeah. Sure do miss Sam."

"You and me both, my friend." Sam was Dr. Samantha Owens, Taylor's best friend and the former head of Forensic Medical, the lead medical examiner for the Mid-State of Tennessee. She'd recently moved to Washington, D.C., and Taylor missed her dreadfully. She understood. God knew she understood. If she'd been faced with the kind of loss Sam experienced, she'd have run away, too. But she couldn't help missing her like hell.

"Have you heard from her?"

"I did, a couple of days ago. She's doing well. Found a place she likes in Georgetown."

"Good. Next time you talk to her, give her my best. I'm going to start running some of the evidence we collected. I'll shout if we get anything that looks relevant."

Taylor glanced at her watch—5:15 p.m. The chief would be down here soon. She needed to hurry up and get him some info he could use for a presser. The chief did so love to be on air, and if they hurried, he could make the 6:00 news.

Keri McGee was on her knees next to the body. Taylor joined her.

"Yo," Keri said.

"Yo back. What do you have for me?"

"A whole lot of nothing. No trauma to the body, outside of the stab wound, of course. I'm about finished here,

54

actually. She's only been dead for a little while, no more than an hour. She was found quickly. Was she living on the streets?"

"Why do you ask?"

"Newspaper in her shoes and socks. They do that for warmth. And she hasn't bathed in a while. Not that that's any real indication, a bunch of these folks have been camping down here for days."

Taylor took her own inventory of Go-Go. That the girl hadn't bathed recently was quite evident. She looked like she'd been living rough: her skin was brown with dirt, she had no jewelry on, no watch, just a small red thread tied around her right wrist. From her matted hair to her grubby clothes, Go-Go was downright filthy. She didn't look much like the other protestors, who, despite their attempts to blend in, still glowed with health.

"I want to talk to whoever found her."

"Over there," Keri said, pointing at a young man who was hovering nearby. "I'm about ready to take her back to the morgue. Fox will autopsy her in the morning, along with everyone else we loaded up on today."

"Sounds good. Thanks."

Taylor took her turn with the kid who'd found the body next. He couldn't be a day over twenty, with a snippet of a beard, dark hair and dark eyes, shoulders hunched into a hooded North Face fleece. Taylor appreciated the irony. The kid was protesting capitalism wearing a two-hundred-dollar jacket. His face was streaked with tears.

"Hey there. I'm Lieutenant Jackson, homicide. What's your name?"

"Derek Rucka."

"How do you know Go-Go?"

"She's my girlfriend."

"Really? You're dating? She doesn't seem to be in very good shape for a girl with a man."

He looked down. "She *was* my girlfriend. We broke up a

few weeks ago. She took off, and I hadn't seen her until today. I was down here with the gang and I saw her smoking on the steps. We chatted."

"About what?"

"Her coming home. She, well, if you know her name, you know her history. Go-Go is bipolar. She's been doing really well, too, working for her dad. That's where we met. My mom is on dialysis. But she stopped taking her meds about a month ago, and things went downhill pretty quickly."

"So you were out here trying to save her?"

He shook his head miserably. "No. Not at all. I didn't know she was out here. I certainly didn't know she was on the streets. I'd have come looking sooner."

"So today of all days, you just happen to run into her, and then boom, she's dead? Is there something you want to tell me, Derek?"

The boy's face flushed with horror, and his mouth dropped open. "What? No. I didn't do anything to her. We just talked. Shared a bowl. That's it."

"So you admit to doing drugs with the deceased?"

The kid nodded, his head moving vigorously on its slender stalk. "Yeah. But I promise, that's all we did."

"I think you should probably come down to my office and talk to me some more, Derek. Okay?"

The bowed shoulders straightened and the tears stopped. His voice grew cold. "Am I under arrest?"

"Not right now. We're just going to have a little chat."

"I know my rights. You can't detain me unless you have cause."

Taylor narrowed her eyes at the boy.

"Don't give me a reason, kid. I'm not in the mood. We can do this hard, or we can do this easy. You just admitted to using an illegal substance on state property. You want to go down on a drug charge, I'm happy to make that happen for you. Or you can come in and have a nice friendly chat. Your call."

She stepped back a foot and fingered her cuffs. Rucka swallowed and shoved his hands in his pockets, head cast downward in defeat.

"Okay then. Come with me." Taylor led the kid to her car, put him in the back seat. "I'll be back in a minute. You just hang out."

Of course, one of the reporters saw this, and shouted across the tape at Taylor frantically. "Lieutenant, do you have a suspect in custody?"

Taylor ignored her. She wasn't about to get in a conversation with a reporter, not when the chief was on his way. No sense stealing the old man's glory. She returned to the body, watched as Keri McGee took samples and bagged the girl's hands.

"Anything?" Taylor asked.

"Not really. Nothing that's leaping out. I have hairs that don't match the body, debris, but that's not a surprise, considering she's out in the crowd like this. She's wrapped up like she's wearing a sari. I'll get her back to the morgue, and we can get her peeled down to her skin, run everything and see what's out of place."

One of these things is not like the other...

Oh, great. Now she was going to be singing that stupid song for the rest of the night.

Taylor didn't blame Keri for wanting to get the girl out of the limelight as quickly as possible, especially with the chief on the way. It was practically record speed for a homicide investigation, but Keri was a stellar death investigator. Taylor trusted her to know when it was time to move on to the next step.

Go-Go would be posted in the morning, along with any other unfortunates who found their way to the tables of Forensic Medical. In the meantime, Taylor had a job to do. She'd started toward the perimeter when Keri shouted to her.

Taylor turned and saw Keri waving her back.

"What's up?"

Keri handed Taylor a small leather wallet. "Found it under her layers of blanket. Don't know why I didn't see it when I rolled her."

"Hers?"

"Not unless her name is James Gustafson."

Taylor flipped the wallet open. It was all the standard stuff: a driver's license and a few credit cards, plus some cash. The photo showed a pale man, forty-one, blue on brown, five foot ten inches. His address showed him to be from Virginia.

"Keri, tell me if I'm crazy. Maybe we just caught a break, and this is our killer's wallet. Go-Go tried picking his pocket, he got pissed and stabbed her, then was spooked and ran before he retrieved it?"

"Would you leave your wallet if you had just stabbed someone?"

"No one said these guys were geniuses."

Keri laughed, then a frown crossed her face. She had her purple-nitrile-gloved hands in the grubby folds of Go-Go's blankets. "Ick. Now that's weird."

"What?" Taylor asked.

Keri produced three more wallets, all very similar to the first, and four cell phones.

"Well, well, well," Taylor said. "Our Go-Go is quite the little pick-pocket."

"Bet there's some folks up on the plaza who will be happy to get their stuff back."

"No kidding. Good job, Keri. I'll have Parks Jr. do some canvassing, see which phone and wallet belongs to which person. They can all come in and have a chat. At least we have some suspects. Maybe we can crack this one tonight. Later, 'gator."

Taylor headed back to the perimeter tape, planning out the evening, and trying to formulate exactly what she was going to say to Go-Go's father about his wayward, now dead daughter.

What a damn shame.

Chapter 5

"Whoo-eeeee!"

Stover had decided to ride the mechanical bull at the Cadillac Ranch. He was spinning in circles, whooping and hollering and generally making an ass of himself. Two bleached blond bimbos had attached themselves to him about an hour earlier, and they gazed adoringly at their man for the evening, salivating over his generosity and the size of his wallet.

JR couldn't stand this much longer. He glanced at his watch; it was past midnight. When had that happened? Granted, he'd been drinking. Keeping up with Stover was a challenge for a man who generally didn't allow himself to indulge in more than the occasional adult beverage, and only then as a reward. Funny, he'd broken his own rules twice in a month. What did that say? Was he getting lax? Tired? Old?

No. Never old. Not in that way. He was certainly aging, like any normal person would, but he was far from staid and predictable.

Stover, now he was predictable. Out of town, away from his wife—and his mistress—looking to grab the first piece of tail that would bite, throw back as much drink as his protruding gut would allow, then fuck and pass out in a strange room without a second thought.

JR was better than that. Cleaner. Seemlier. And certainly more temperate. Stover drew attention to himself like a five-year-old throwing a tantrum—everyone around was aware of him. JR never could handle that level of attention from strangers. Not that he wanted to. God, if he were this indiscreet, he'd have landed in a jail cell years ago. No, prudence and moderation were the keys to his longevity.

Almost as if Stover could read his mind, the man started yelling in a drunken slur. "JR." The name came out *Jar*. "Ca'mere. Get yer bony ass up here."

The blondes twittered and simpered.

JR waved him off, then realized how incredibly intoxicated Stover was. After his invitation, he'd closed his eyes and started to slide off the back of the bull.

It was time to go.

He turned and walked to the bar to settle the bill. Stover had given the bartender his credit card to hold to keep the tab open. JR asked for the tab, and told the bartender to keep it on the card. He figured Stover might as well pay for the drinks, considering how inconsiderate he was being.

But the bartender came back and told JR the card had been declined. Cursing silently, he reached for his own wallet. He'd just give the man some cash, and be done with it.

His back right pocket was empty.

Son of a bitch.

He glanced over to the women who'd latched on to them, but couldn't see either of them in the crowd.

Fury began to build in his chest, so hard and fast that the bartender reared back when he saw the look on JR's face. He'd been ripped off. The worthless bitches had stolen his wallet and run.

He went to Stover, who'd just tripped off the bull, and grabbed him by the shirtfront.

JR hissed the words. "They stole my wallet, you fat fuck."

"Sucks for you." Stover began to laugh, the hysterical giggles of a drunken hyena, which just pissed JR off more. He dragged the man to the bar, pushed him roughly against the wooden rail.

"Your card was declined. Pay the tab."

Something in JR's voice registered with Stover. He obeyed immediately, pulled his wallet out—he still had his, the shit—and paid for their drinks with two crisp $100 bills.

Satisfied, JR stalked away. He needed to find those women. The last thing he wanted was his name getting out. Granted, it wasn't his real name on the license and credit cards, but a variation, a pseudonym, if you will, something he used to assure his anonymity as he cruised the country. He'd adopted the name when he failed out of med school. Employers wouldn't be inclined to hire a man who they perceived wasn't even competent enough to finish school. That wasn't it, wasn't it at all. He could have done the work if he wanted to, but he'd found another hobby, one that satisfied him in ways being a doctor never would. He made a show of struggling with the work so his classmates would think he was just incapable, and he could fade away from their lives.

But Stover was his Achilles heel. He knew JR's real name. The idiot had spied him in the hotel in New Orleans and remembered.

JR pulled up short at the door to the street. The women became secondary. That was a problem, but it wasn't fatal. He knew what he needed to do. There was only one way to really fix this mess.

Stover had to die.

He felt a tingle of excitement go through his body.

Two in one day? In one city? Dare he?

His mind answered in the affirmative, with a caveat.

Don't use the knife.

JR waited for Stover to catch up to him, his mind racing. So many ways to die. Fall in front of a car, trip and hit your

61

head on a light pole...

He thought about his drive around the city earlier and it hit him. The river was only a block away. There were three bridges, too, one of which was solely for pedestrians.

JR assessed the man beside him. He was drunk enough. He'd never be able to swim.

It wouldn't have the satisfaction of the knife—nothing could top that—but this would solve one very large, loud, nagging problem.

He turned to his old friend.

"Come on, Heath. Let's go for a walk."

Stover fell into step beside him, yammering away. God, did the man ever shut his trap?

Well, JR, give him this. It is his last will and testament, after all.

It only took five minutes to mount the bridge and cross halfway to the highest point. He stopped to admire the view. They were standing over the murky river water, the lights of Nashville shining majestically in the darkness.

Time to say goodbye.

He didn't mean to do it. He really didn't. JR gave Stover a push, and the drunken fool began to struggle, and there was nothing to be done for it. The blade was in his hand before he even gave it a second thought. JR shoved the knife in quickly, then drew it out. The pain was enough to stop Stover's cries. He didn't move for a moment, looking vaguely surprised, then toppled over the edge of the bridge himself, with no effort whatsoever.

JR did something he'd only done once before, in another moment of extreme distress. He tossed the knife off the bridge after Stover's body. It killed him to do it—my God, what a prize for his collection, a blade that took not one, but two lives, in a single day—but he'd been forced into impulsivity here in Nashville, and like any animal who knew it had just survived a close call, he needed to retreat to his bolt hole and lick his wounds.

He would call the conference organizers first thing in the morning and plead a bad case of food poisoning. In the meantime, he needed to cut his losses and get the hell out of Dodge.

Nashville had been a little too good to him.

Chapter 6

Taylor spent Monday evening keeping the wheels in motion on Go-Go's murder. She had a long, sad chat with Joe Dunham, promised him she'd do everything in her power to bring Go-Go's killer to justice as quickly as possible. It wasn't an empty promise; she had several solid leads already. She was confident she'd have her man soon.

Derek Rucka's interrogation gave her absolutely squat, outside of the fact that Go-Go had been known to suffer from a wee bit of kleptomania, and going off her meds had exacerbated the syndrome. She was a pack rat, indiscriminately lifting whatever she could get her hands on: wallets and phones mostly, but brushes, lipsticks, pens—anything that could be separated from its owner. According to Rucka, it was purely for fun; she took a perverse pleasure in getting away with it.

The kid's story checked out, and a canvas of the protestors confirmed that he was on the other side of the memorial when Go-Go went down. Taylor cut him loose just after midnight.

They'd also found all the wallet and cell phone owners, save one: Gustafson. Everyone else checked out. Taylor had that niggling feeling in the back of her head that there was something to this guy. It was something in his eyes. Alone at her desk, she stared at his license photo for a few minutes, then ran him through the system. Clean. She found a phone number and called, but the phone just rang and rang and rang.

Instinct is vital for every homicide detective, and hers was on fire. She called the local precinct that serviced the area where Gustafson lived in Virginia, but it was late, and they were busy working their own cases. Someone would get back to her tomorrow, supposedly. She knew well enough that she'd have to call back in the morning, made a note of it on her list.

She'd lock him down tomorrow. Frustrated, she headed home.

John Baldwin, her fiancé, an FBI profiler, was in Minnesota working a case, so Taylor had the house to herself. Sleep never came easy for her, with or without Baldwin's presence, but she'd grown accustomed to having him in her bed while she gazed at the ceiling, at the very least to warm her chilly feet. With both he and Sam gone, she was a bit lonely. But instead of wallowing, she grabbed a beer from the fridge, racked up a game of nine-ball and expertly shot the balls down one by one, until she finally began to weary around three. She slept a couple of fitful hours, then got up, showered and headed to Forensic Medical for Go-Go's autopsy.

Taylor attended herself so the chief could have instant updates to share with his high profile friends. It was an unremarkable event and only served to make her miss Sam more. Dr. Fox was a good ME, quick and to the point, but he lacked that little bit extra, the sixth sense Sam seemed to have for making a murder come to life. The girl had been stabbed once, the knife most likely a seven-to-eight-inch, double-bladed stiletto, sliding right past her ribs, under her breastbone, and into her heart. THC showed on the tox screen; a more complete report would take weeks. Exsanguination was the official cause of death, and it was ruled a homicide.

Taylor felt sorry for Go-Go. She was obviously a very troubled girl, but not one who deserved to die on the street at the wrong end of a blade.

It was still early when Fox finished the post. Taylor debated stopping at Waffle House and getting breakfast, but decided to go back to the office first, which ended up being a good call. The videos from TPAC were waiting on her, with a note from Tim: "Check out 3:47 p.m. Think we may have a shot of our guy. I'm in court, will be over as soon as I'm done."

Taylor popped the disc into her laptop and hit Play.

The footage was surprisingly clear, though in muted black and white. She dragged the bar to the spot Tim suggested and hit play. It took three replays to see it. Damn, Tim had a good eye. There was a flash of white in the bottom right edge of the screen, which Taylor figured must be the bill of a hat. Her theory was confirmed a moment later when a man walked through the full frame, wearing a white baseball cap. He stepped right into a bundle of rags that Taylor assumed must have been Go-Go, then disappeared out of the frames. Go-Go dropped to the ground, and that was it. A fraction of a second. And the bastard's back to the camera the whole time.

Well, the tapes had at least narrowed her search down to the male species. That cut out fifty percent of the suspect pool.

She did some quick mental measuring, putting the guy against the stone wall that led to the auditorium and figured he wasn't over six feet. That Gustafson fellow was about that height as well.

She played the tape several more times, but couldn't find anything more. The idea that Go-Go had managed to pick the man's pocket as he stabbed her looked incredibly remote. It was a blitz attack, fast, clean. Professional even. And if it was his wallet, he certainly didn't attempt to retrieve it. He hit the girl, knocked her down and was gone in the blink of an eye.

Maybe Taylor was barking up the wrong tree here.

Her phone rang, interrupting her thoughts, and she glanced down to see the cell number of her new sergeant. She answered, "Jackson."

"Hey, Loot. It's Parks. I'm down here on River Road boat ramp. We have a floater. ID on him says his name is Heath Stover, late of the Big Easy."

"Bully for you. Call Wade, he's on. I'm working Go-Go."

Parks said, "I know you are. I've already got Wade here. But this is something you might want to see. Our New Orleans dude? He's been stabbed. Right in the same spot as Go-Go."

Chapter 7

Heath Stover's overweight torso bore a familiar mark, just under his sternum, a slash in the flesh that allowed the yellow subcutaneous fat to squish out around the edges of the wound. The water had washed the blood away. Fox got on the autopsy immediately once the body arrived at Forensic Medical, and Taylor stood to the side, watching, arms crossed, tapping the toe of her boot on the floor while Fox measured and murmured and inserted a special ruler into the slit to determine its depth. He finally stood and nodded.

"Same kind of blade. Double edged, sharp as hell. See how there's no hesitation, or wiggle room? Went straight in, under the sternum and into the heart." Fox stood up and looked at Taylor, his brown eyes troubled. "I have to tell you, Lieutenant, whoever did this knew what he was doing."

"Is it the same person who killed Go-Go?"

"I can't tell you that. But he—or she—knew exactly where to place the blade for maximum effectiveness. This isn't your everyday stabbing. It's clean, precise, and done with amazing skill. And Go-Go's was exactly the same."

"I think we're safe saying *he*. I believe we have Go-Go's

murder on tape. If she hadn't gone down I'd have thought he just bumped into her. It was quick. Here, help me run this through."

They played out the scenario she'd seen on the tape a few times, and Fox confirmed that based on Go-Go's wound, the stabbing could definitely work the way Taylor had seen on the videotape.

Fox turned back to his newest guest. "But Stover here, he got stabbed, then went in the river somewhere. Wasn't in the water too long, and there is water in his lungs, just a bit. He was on his last legs when he went in, but he was alive. Could be your blitz attacker hit him and he went in the water, or he killed him by the bank and pushed him over the edge. Radiographs show he does have a few broken bones, so he either got in a fight, or fell—"

Taylor stopped tapping her foot. "Off one of the bridges. That would explain the broken bones. We can do a current analysis from last night, see where he might have gone into the river."

"That makes sense to me. Huh. If this is the same killer, he did two in one day. Dude's got a serious problem."

"No kidding. Thanks, Fox. Now I have to go put Stover and Go-Go together, find out what they have in common. Then I can figure out who did this to them both."

The words floated to her head again, this time slightly altered.

One of these things is too much like the other.

Chapter 8

Taylor spent the drive back to the office in deep thought. Two kills, exactly alike, with two people who, on the surface, had absolutely nothing in common. A quick investigation on Stover found that he was in town on business, had checked into the Hermitage Hotel in the late afternoon, asked directions to Rippy's BBQ on Broadway, then, around six the previous evening, set off on foot toward LoBro. Marcus Wade was down there now, nosing around. Hopefully there'd be a lead.

In the meantime, Taylor set to work getting in touch with the Fairfax County Police in Virginia. A few annoying false starts later, she was finally connected to a detective named Drake Hagerman. Taylor laid out the story and asked for his help tracking down Gustafson. He promised to get back to her within the day. Satisfied, Taylor hung up and called Marcus to see what was shaking on his end.

What was shaking, apparently, was pay dirt. Marcus answered in a huff.

"I was just about to call you. Can you send me a picture of the guy whose wallet Go-Go had, the one we didn't find last night?"

"I'll bring it down myself. Why? You got something?"

"Stover was in here last night, dining with another guy. Description sounds an awful lot like that photo on the license. If it's him... "

Taylor felt that flash of excitement she got when a case was about to break wide open. Less than twenty-four hours. Impressive. Her people were damn good at their jobs.

"I'll be there in five."

She called Chief DeMike and let him know what was happening, then set off down to Rippy's.

The bar was packed full, the lunch crowd rolling in food and drink and overly loud country music. Taylor would love to know how much they pulled down in a year; Rippy's was always packed to the gills.

She found Marcus at the back bar, chatting with a ponytailed, jean-clad waitress. He looked quite pleased with himself. Marcus was adorable, and his good looks sometimes helped loosen tongues. Taylor gave him a look; he cleared his throat and became completely professional.

"Lieutenant, Brandy served Mr. Stover last night. She said he was with another gentleman."

Taylor pulled a six-pack of photos she'd put together out of her jack-et pocket and handed it to the waitress. "Do any of these men look familiar to you?"

Gustafson was on the top row, third photo.

Brandy didn't hesitate.

"That's the guy," she said, pointing to Gustafson.

"You're one-hundred-percent certain?"

"Absolutely. Gave me the creeps. He smiled too much. And didn't tip. They were going honky-tonking. The fat one asked me the best place to go. I sent them to Tootsies, of course, and suggested the Cadillac Ranch, too."

Taylor met Marcus's eye. "Thank you, ma'am. Please keep this to yourself. You may be called on again to provide information. Are you willing to do that?"

"I am. If he's a creep, I don't want him back in here. Hey, I

71

gotta go. My manager's giving me the evil eye." She glanced coquettishly at Marcus. "Shout at me sometime."

Marcus blushed red, and Taylor gave him a smile.

"You're such a charmer."

"You know it. So this is our guy, huh?"

"Looks that way. You keep on this trail, see if you can nail down exactly what might have happened. I'm rather amazed, actually. Either this guy dropped his wallet while he was stabbing Go-Go, or she managed to slide it out of his pocket. Pretty incredible presence of mind for a girl who's stoned and dying."

"But she was an accomplished pickpocket. Maybe she targeted him just as he targeted her. And they both got screwed."

Taylor nodded. "That makes sense. Well done, Go-Go. She practically handed us her killer on a platter. I'm heading back to the office and hitting up the Internets."

"All right. See you later."

Taylor watched Marcus stride away, thankful to have his keen investigative mind at her disposal, then walked back to her vehicle. She had a date with a computer.

The email notification on her iPhone chimed just as she turned the engine over. It was Hagerman, from Fairfax County. According to him, there was no one named James Gustafson in the Virginia DMV system, and the address on the license was a vacant lot. Her killer was a ghost.

NOVELLA IN 3 PARTS

Chapter 9

ViCAP, the Violent Criminal Apprehension Program, could be a homicide detective's best friend, if they knew exactly how to use it. It wasn't as easy as inputting your crime and the system spitting out a match to similar crimes. You had to know what to ask for. Taylor had unfortunately availed herself of its services many times in the past, and had the level of expertise needed to run the appropriate request chain into the queue. Hopefully the results would come back quickly, but the service wasn't fully automated. A real person had to do some of the legwork, and the FBI was backed up three ways to Sunday on requests. So she inputted the parameters, taking great care with the specifics of both Go-Go's and Heath Stover's murders—the exactness of the stab wounds, all the similarities she could find—crossed her fingers, and went on to the next component of her investigation: figuring out who this Gustafson man really was.

The ViCAP results came back several hours later, much quicker than she expected. She read the email in her inbox with trepidation, then sat back in her chair, let the realization wash over her. There were matches in the system from several places around the country, the most recent a homeless woman in New Orleans. Gustafson, whoever the son of a bitch really was, had been a busy, busy boy.

Taylor knew it was time to start raising the red flags. Too many jurisdictions, too many victims. She filled the chief in on her plan, got an *atta-girl*, then went to the source. Her fiancé was a profiler, after all.

Baldwin answered on the first ring. "Hey, love. How are you?"

"Hi, babe. I've been better. Two unsolved cases on my desk from yesterday alone, and just got a report back from ViCAP. I think I've got a serial on my hands." She gave him all the details, then emailed him the ViCAP report. She waited while he accessed it and read the findings. A few minutes later, he agreed.

"You might be right," he said. "What did you say this guy's name is again?"

"The license said James Gustafson, but Fairfax County just confirmed that no one by that name exists in the system, and the address is a fake. The license, the cards, all of it, they're either excellent identity theft or really sophisticated forgeries. Who is this guy?"

"An excellent question."

"My theory is he's been killing off the radar for years. And he broke his MO with this latest victim. He's been preying on homeless until now. Go-Go was a fuck up, she certainly looked the part, but hitting a well-established surgeon from New Orleans? One mistake could be an accident, sure, but the other... there's a tie to his past, I'm sure of it. The waitress got the impression they two men were friends, out for a night on the town. Maybe Stover knew the real identity of the killer, and Gustafson felt threatened."

"That's a solid theory. He killed a different type of victim out of sequence. The back-to-back kills, I'd bet he's in some sort of trouble and is decompensating."

"Well, he's screwed up. Now we know about him. He's on

the radar, and I'm about to make his world hell."

"He sounds like someone who has spent his life being very, very careful. Listen, I'm totally wrapped up in this case, or else I'd help you myself. But I know who to call. I've worked with her on cases before. She's sharp. I think you should have a chat with her."

"What's her name?"

"Maggie O'Dell. Hold on a sec, let me get her number for you." He rattled off the numbers and she wrote them down.

"I'll call her right now. Thanks, honey. Call me later, okay?"

"Will do. Love you."

"Love you, too."

Taylor hung up the phone, waited a moment, then dialed. Even if O'Dell couldn't help, at least the FBI would be aware that something was hinky with the so-called James Robert Gustafson.

The call went to voicemail. Taylor left a message, told the agent who she was, her connection to Baldwin, that she had a significant ViCAP match and wanted to touch base. She hung up the phone, leaned back in her chair and put her boots on the desk.

She'd get some justice for Go-Go, and for Stover. Their deaths would not go unpunished. No matter what. And for the moment, that was the best she could do.

Epilogue

The lights of Washington, D.C. greeted JR. Luminous, beautiful; the city was home. He always felt secure once he crossed into Fairfax County, knowing he was just miles from his basecamp. It had been a long trip, exhausting in its way, but so, so worth it.

Sated, he was calm again, the fury of the past month's excess slaking the thirst in his blood. Now he would lay low. Fit back into his life. Go to work like a good little boy. Recharge his batteries. Maybe a small vacation, somewhere in the mountains, where he could watch the snow fall, listen to birds chirp and water run and feel the cool air pass over his skin.

And remember. *Always, always remember.*

NEW YORK TIMES BESTSELLING AUTHOR

ALEX KAVA

COLD METAL NIGHT

OMAHA, NEBRASKA

Chapter 1

Sunday, December 4
2:37 a.m.
Downtown Omaha, Nebraska

Nick Morelli stuffed his hands deep inside his pockets.

Damn! It had gotten cold.

And he'd forgotten his gloves. He could see his breath. Air so cold it stung his eyes and hurt to breathe.

Snow crunched beneath his shoes. Italian leather. Salvatore Ferragamo slip-ons. Five hundred and ten dollars. The stupidest purchase he'd ever let his sister, Christine talk him into. They made him look like a mob boss, or worse – a politician – instead of a security expert.

He was at a private party when he got Pete's call. Figured he could easily walk the two blocks from the Flat Iron to the Rockwood Building. But it had been snowing steadily for the last ten hours. Now he treaded carefully over the pile of ice chunks the snowplows left at the curbs. He already almost wiped out twice despite the salt and sand.

City crews were working overtime, trying to clear the streets for Sunday's Holiday of Lights Festival. It was a huge celebration. The beginning of the Christmas season. Live music, carolers, art and craft events. Performers dressed as

Dickens characters would stroll the Old Market's cobblestone streets. The ConAgra Ice Rink would be packed with skaters. Tomorrow night the city would turn on tens of thousands of twinkling white lights that decorated all the trees on the Gene Leahy Mall and strung along the rooftops of the downtown buildings. Even the high-rises.

A festive time and a security nightmare for people like Nick. The company he worked for, United Allied, provided security for a dozen buildings in the area. The Rockwood Building was one of them.

As Nick hurried across Sixteenth Street he glanced up to see the fat, wet flakes glitter against the night sky. It was the kind of stuff he and his sister called magical Christmas dust when they were kids.

Pete was waiting for him at the back door of the Rockwood Building. It was one of Nick's favorites. A historic brick six-story with an atrium in the middle that soared up all six floors. Reminded Nick of walking into an indoor garden, huge green plants and a domed skylight above. The building housed offices, all of them quiet at this time of night, making Pete's job more about caretaking than guarding.

But tonight Pete looked spooked. His eyes were wide. His hair looked a shade whiter against his black skin. He held a nightstick tight in his trembling hands. Nick had never seen the old man like this. He didn't even know Pete owned a nightstick.

"He didn't show up at midnight like usual," Pete was telling Nick as he led him down a hallway. Nick wasn't sure who he was talking about. All he told Nick on the phone was, "Please get over here . . . now."

He was taking Nick to another exit, doublewide doors that opened out into an alley. The doors weren't used except by maintenance or housekeeping to haul out the trash.

"He usually stops by. You said it was okay." He shot a look back over his shoulder at Nick but he didn't slow down. "He does a little shoveling if I ask." Pete was out of breath.

The nightstick stayed in his right fist. "I made us some hot cocoa tonight. So cold out. When he didn't show up I took a look around."

Pete shoved open the doors, slow and easy, peeking around them like he was expecting someone to jump out at him.

"Pete, you're starting to freak me out." Nick patted him on the shoulder, gently holding him back so he could step around him. "If someone's in trouble, we'll help him out."

After Thanksgiving he had made an executive decision to allow homeless people to sleep in some of the back entries of the buildings he took care of. He told Pete and his other night guards to call him if there was a problem. During the holidays he didn't have the heart to toss them into the street. Most of them didn't cause any problems. They were just looking for someplace to get out of the cold.

Nick took two steps out into the frigid alley and immediately he saw a heap of gray wool and dirty denim in a bloody pile of snow. The man's face was twisted under a bright green and orange argyle scarf that Nick recognized. His stomach fell to his knees.

"Oh God, not Gino. What the hell happened?"

Nick tried to get closer. The damned shoes slipped on a trail of blood that was already icing over. He lost his balance. Started to fall. His hand caught the corner of the Dumpster. Ice-cold metal sliced open his palm but he held on. By now he was breathing hard. Puffs of steam like a dragon. He took a deep breath, planted his feet. Then he reached over to Gino while still gripping the corner of the Dumpster.

Nick pressed two fingers to the man's neck. Gino's skin was almost as cold as the metal of the Dumpster.

81

Chapter 2

4:45 a.m.
Crown Plaza
Kansas City, Missouri

Salsa music startled Maggie O'Dell awake. She jolt up in bed and scrambled to the edge before she realized it was her phone. She'd accidentally changed the ringtone and had been too exhausted to fix it.

"I think we may have caught a lucky break," the voice said without a greeting.

It was R.J. Tully, her sometimes partner when the FBI sent two instead of one. A rare occasion these days.

She pushed hair out of her eyes, blinked to focus on the red digits of the hotel's alarm clock.

"It better be lucky. You woke me up."

"Aw geez! Sorry. I thought you never sleep."

Tully had to be the only law enforcement officer she knew who said things like "Aw geez and holy crap." It made her smile as she fumbled in the dark to turn on a light.

"Seriously, I didn't think you'd be asleep," he followed up.

He knew she had been battling a stretch of insomnia for over a year now. Getting shot in the head two months ago didn't help matters. Technically it was called a "scraping of the skull alongside the left temporal lobe." Unofficially it hurt like hell and the throbbing pain that still visited her head on a regular basis was a bitch. Otherwise she was okay. At least that's what she kept telling people.

"What's the lucky break?"

"Got a phone call from Omaha. Homeless man. Stabbed. Looks like our guy."

She stood up from the bed, rubbed the sleep from her eyes and started turning on lamps. She'd been in the Kansas City area trying to dig up something, anything. But the victim here, and the evidence, was already two weeks cold.

"What makes them think it's our guy?"

"Blitz attack. No other injuries. Single stab wound to the chest, just under the rib cage. Preliminaries suggest a long, double-edged blade."

That sounded about right.

For four weeks she'd been chasing this guy halfway around the country. It started at the end of October when FBI agent John Baldwin asked her to take a look at a slice 'n go down in Nashville. Maggie was still recovering from her own injuries but she owed Baldwin a favor and told him she'd take a look.

Lieutenant Taylor Jackson had sent Maggie every scrap they had on the case, which included witness interviews, security video and even a driver's license. Unfortunately the video footage showed only a flash of white at the bottom of the screen—the bill of a white ballcap. The driver's license ended up being a deadend, too, although it was an excellent fake. Even the witness interviews didn't turn up anything too interesting except that the man in question "smiled too much."

Just when Maggie believed there wasn't enough to go on something odd happened. Her boss, Assistant Director Raymond Kunze, head of the Behavioral Science Unit at Quantico brought her the case – the exact same case. He insisted she and Tully make it their top priority. Kunze had been sending Tully and her around on wild goose chases for almost a year. Maggie was immediately suspicious. Why this case? What was the political connection? Who did Kunze owe a favor to this time?

She hated that she was right. Turns out the senior senator from Tennessee was a personal friend of the Nashville victim's father. It didn't take much digging for Maggie to discover this wasn't a one-time "slice 'n go." She and Tully had found another two victims in New Orleans. According to NOPD Detective Stacy Killian, both were homeless, one a new mother, the other an elderly man.

Searching ViCAP she discovered what could be as many as ten to twelve victims. Different cities across the country. Similar victims. Same MO. All of them quite possibly the work of one killer she and Tully nicknamed the Night Slicer.

Now Maggie paced the hotel room listening to Tully give her more details. She could hear him rattling paper and knew the notes he had taken were probably on a take-out menu or dry cleaning receipt – his usual notepads, whatever was handy.

"Here's the thing," Tully said. "Omaha's ME thinks this one happened earlier this morning. Internal body temp says within last six hours. Night security guard claims it had to be around two o'clock."

"Two o'clock in the morning? That's only a few hours ago. How can he be so sure?"

"He knows the victim. Says the guy..." more paper shuffling. "Says Gino usually picked up a dozen extras of the Sunday *Omaha World Herald* right off the dock. He'd sell them on the street to make a few bucks. But first, he'd bring the security guard a copy and they'd drink hot chocolate."

"That sounds all very nice but since when do we determine time of death from a security guard's Sunday morning ritual?"

"Thing is, they found him between two-thirty and three this mornin. He already had his dozen newspapers. The

Sunday edition didn't hit the dock until two-o-five."

Tully went silent. He was waiting for it to settle in and Maggie finally understood the lucky break.

"So we've got a fresh kill," she said. And then the realization hit her. "And less than twenty-four hours before he slices number two and leaves town."

"Omaha's about 180 miles from Kansas City. Just a hop up and a skip down. Twenty, thirty minute flight," Tully said. "Might be some delays. Sounds like there's a bunch of new snow."

"I have a rental. I'll drive." She hated flying. Tully's "hop up and skip down" already had her stomach flipping. "It'll probably be quicker than trying to get a flight, getting to the airport, going through security."

"Looks like a three hour drive, but in the snow—"

"No problem."

"You sure?"

"You worry too much. I'll exchange my rental car for an SUV. Let Omaha know I'm on my way."

Chapter 3

5:41 a.m.
Old Market Embassy Suites
Omaha

He looked down out his suite's window and down on the empty cobblestoned streets. Earlier there had been horses and carriages, street performers on a couple of the corners. The brick buildings used to be warehouses on the Missouri River but now housed restaurants and specialty shops.

Last night despite the snow, the sidewalks had been filled with people, the streets busy with traffic. There had even been a patrol officer on horseback. And yet just five, six blocks away he been able to slide a blade up into a man's heart and walk away. In fact, he walked back through the hustle and bustle to his hotel without a single person noticing.

All was good. He was back in his groove. That nagging fury would no longer drive him to make reckless mistakes.

New Orleans had set him off track. Then Nashville really screwed him up. He had always been careful about choosing targets no one would miss. But Heath Stover, a blast from the past, had knocked him way off his game. And so did that girl, that rich bitch pretending to be some lost soul. The news media continued to cover her murder but at least they were calling it just another unfortunate incident. Just another of a long list of crimes besieging the Occupy camps across the country.

That's the word a reporter used, "besieging," like the protesters were soldiers in dugouts coming under attack. He shook his head at that. He was sick of seeing the protesters in every city he traveled to. Thankfully he hadn't had to deal with any of them in Kansas City or here in Omaha. Another good sign that he was finally back on track.

And why shouldn't he be back on top of the world? Sales were up. Bosco's new laser-guided scalpel was a huge hit. Omaha's medical mecca was like putty in his hands on Thursday and Friday at the Quest Center conference. He had exploded past his sales quota.

Still, it had taken this morning's kill to completely renew his confidence.

He looked around the suite and rubbed his hands together. Checked his watch. Maybe he would shower, dress and go down for the breakfast buffet. He had the whole day off. He didn't have to leave until tomorrow morning. Tonight he was looking forward to the Holiday of Lights festivities. The Old Market would be filled with people again and sounds of the seasons. Now with his newfound confidence he wouldn't need to go far at all to find target number two.

Chapter 4

7:59 a.m.
Omaha Police Headquarters

Nick Morrelli crushed the paper cup and tossed it into the corner wastebasket. He'd had enough coffee. He was tired. He wanted to go home. He rubbed his eyes and paced the room, a poor excuse for an employee lounge with a metal table and folding chairs, a row of vending machines, coffee maker and a sagging sofa along the back wall.

The door opened and his captor came in, shirtsleeves rolled up, shaved head shiny with perspiration. Detective Tommy Pakula handed Nick a black and white printout. It was a copy of a driver's license.

"Do you recognize this guy? Maybe seen him around any of your properties?"

The license had been enlarged which only made the photo blurred. The guy looked pretty ordinary, could be anybody.

"No, I don't think so."

Pakula sat down in one of the folding chairs. Pointed to one across the table for Nick to sit down. They'd already done this. What more could he ask? But Nick sat down. Tommy Pakula was one of the good guys. Four daughters. Still married to his high school sweetheart. Nick had been questioned by him before a couple years ago. Another case. Another killer.

"You were a sheriff not so long ago," Pakula said, getting Nick's attention.

That was true. Nick had been a county sheriff. Got his fill after a killer almost claimed his nephew as his next victim.

Just when Nick thought Pakula might finally cut him some slack, the man came in with another verbal punch. "You should know better. So tell me again why you thought you should be touching this dead guy before you called us?"

"If he wasn't dead I wanted to help him."

Pakula raised an eyebrow.

"It's Gino," Nick said in almost a whisper.

He watched Pakula sit back, pull in a long deep breath. Rubbed his jaw.

Everybody loved Gino. Nobody knew his last name but he was a familiar face downtown, part of the landscape. Years ago he used to sell Italian sausage and peppers out of a rickety stand he'd set up on the corner of Sixteenth and Douglas, right in front of the Brandeis Building. Suddenly he was living on the streets. Tall, thin—a little bent over, as he grew older—with friendly brown eyes that sparkled despite his situation. Security guards, police officers, even the guys on the newspaper's loading dock gave him twelve papers every Sunday morning for him to sell and buy himself a hot breakfast that wasn't one provided by a local shelter. They all loved Gino. Took care of him. But they hadn't taken care of him last night.

"Is this the guy you think stabbed Gino?" Nick held up the printout.

Pakula nodded. "FBI thinks so, too. He's done it in other cities. We've been keeping an eye out ever since he hit Kansas City about two weeks ago."

"Mind if I keep this?"

"Go ahead. Maybe check with your security people. You

said your company has how many buildings downtown?"

"Nine. Plus three in the Old Market."

Nick folded the printout. Tucked it in the back pocket of his trousers. He'd get this bastard himself if he had to. Then he tried to decide if he should tell Pakula that the Rockwood Building had security cameras on every corner. Before he decided, the door to the lounge opened again and a young cop stuck his head inside.

"Sorry to interrupt. A woman's here to see you, Detective Pakula. Insisted I tell you that she brought you doughnuts all the way from Kansas City?"

The young cop's face flushed a bit, like he wasn't sure if he should be delivering what sounded like a personal message.

Pakula smiled and stood up. "Send her in here."

The cop disappeared. Pakula shot Nick a look. Another smile.

"FBI," he said. "First time I met her I was eating a doughnut. Had a cup of coffee in my other hand." He shook his head, but grin hadn't left yet. "She'll never stop busting my chops about that."

Nick should have figured it out, but he was totally surprised when the lounge door opened again and Maggie O'Dell walked in, carrying a white bakery box that she meant as a joke for Pakula. From the look on her face when she saw Nick, he figured the joke was probably on her. But only for a second or two.

"Nick Morrelli," she said. "I haven't seen you since you drove off with that blonde bomb expert in Minneapolis."

Nick winced. *Damn, she was good.*

Chapter 5

10:57 a.m.
The Rockwood Building

The last time Maggie had worked with Nick Morrelli they spent hours watching security footage. Mall of America. The day after Thanksgiving. Black Friday became bloody Friday. Three college kids set off backpacks filled with explosives.

Here they were again, sitting in a small room in front of a wall of computer monitors.

"How's Timmy and Christine?" she asked. She and Nick had history that went back further than Minneapolis. They'd worked on a serial killer case when Nick was sheriff. And again, years later when the killer returned.

"Timmy's playing football this year. Christine's good."

They sat side by side in captain's chairs like pilots in a cockpit. Pakula would join them in a half hour or so.

"How's your doctor?" Nick asked, keeping his eyes on the computer monitors but unsuccessful in keeping the sarcasm out of his voice.

Instead of telling him that Benjamin Platt was not hers, she simply said, "Ben's good."

She refrained from asking whatever happened to the blonde bomb expert. That was over a year ago. She knew

Nick probably didn't remember the woman's name anymore. And there lied the reason that she had never seriously considered a relationship with Nick Morrelli. Simply put—he wasn't relationship material. Maggie had too drama in er professional life to put up with it in her personal life.

But charming, yes. Handsome—God, he was still gorgeous. Tall, dark and handsome with blue eyes. He had managed to keep his college quarterback physique. She didn't deny that there had been chemistry between the two of them. Just sitting next to him she could still feel it. Annoying as hell.

She tried to turn her attention to the monitors. She was exhausted from lack of sleep. Her back was tight and tense from a slippery three-hour drive in a small rental car because everyone else had the good sense of renting the SUV's before the snow hit. Somehow she needed to focus.

She pulled up the chair. Planted her elbows on the table in front of her.

"Who are you this week?" she said aloud to the computer monitor, like the Night Slicer might answer.

"Pakula gave me a copy of the driver's license."

"That's all we have."

"You think he changes his appearance?"

"He must, but I'm guessing it's subtle. He definitely changes his name. He has a normal life somewhere. I think he travels the country on business. Different cities. A new group of people each time who don't know him. We have that picture from the driver's license out to every metropolitan police department. We haven't gotten a hit yet."

"But you've been tracking him?"

"Only by his victims. And his M.O. He's right-handed. Uses a double-blade stiletto. At least seven inches long. He does a blitz attack. It's probably no more than an incidental bump. Slips the blade in just under the breastbone where he knows he won't have any bone chattering. The angle of the knife is interesting."

"So somehow he knows exactly where to stab?"

"Yes, it appears so."

She glanced at Nick while he tapped buttons on a keyboard. He started the film footage from a camera labeled: Northwest corner of Rockwood.

"His image was captured on a security camera at the Tennessee Performing Arts Center," Maggie continued. "Actually it was only his back but it was enough to give us some idea of how tall he is compared to his victim. He has to angle the blade—"

She pushed out her chair and stood. "It's probably easier if I show you." Fact was she was too exhausted to talk about it. He glanced up at her, paused the monitors and stood up in front of her.

She grabbed a ballpoint pen from the table and held it in her right hand the same way she believed the Night Slicer did.

"He holds it low. Probably has the stiletto up his sleeve until he needs it." She stepped closer. "He always slips it in just below the rib cage." She put her left hand flat against Nick's abdomen to show him where and immediately she realized this was a mistake when she felt him shiver under her touch. Her eyes met his and she felt the heat rush to her face.

Thankfully exhaustion pushed her into professional mode. She took a step back as she moved her hand with the pen and her arm in the same motion the killer must use.

"He shoves the knife in at an upward angle. Usually pierces the heart. Sometimes the lungs. Sometimes both."

Finished with the show and tell, she avoided his eyes and took her seat again. Waited for him to do the same. He was slow about joining her and she wanted to kick herself. There was obvious still too much between them. She glanced over at him. Wanted to tell him she couldn't afford any of the emotion she was seeing in his face right now.

"Gino was a good guy," he said, surprising her. "He didn't

deserve to die this way."

She was wrong. The emotion wasn't about her. Maybe she was a little disappointed that it wasn't about her.

"He's been killing two victims in each city. Usually within a period of twenty-four hours." Maggie sat back. Ran her fingers through her hair. "Then he disappears. Gone. Like he never existed." She looked at her wristwatch. "In less than fifteen hours he's going to kill someone else."

Chapter 6

1:39 p.m.
The Old Market

He had been watching the old woman for over an hour. He followed her around but kept to the shadows and back far enough away that she never noticed him. Though he wondered if she noticed much of anything around her.

He'd gotten close enough to hear her muttering. Not just talking to herself but arguing as if with some invisible friend. She had abandoned her shopping cart behind a Dumpster, tucking it away to hide it as best as she could. The snow made it too difficult for her to move it over the crusted piles left by the snowplows. He almost helped her once. Wanting to touch the fringe of her gray knit hat and feel whether the fringe was part of the hat or actually her hair.

Her territory seemed to be within the Old Market area. Interesting, since he didn't see any other homeless people here, venturing around the cobble-stoned district. He watched as she wandered the streets quite fascinated by things no one else saw. Once he saw her stop abruptly in the middle of the sidewalk and wave pedestrians around her to avoid stepping on something smashed in the snow. No one else stopped to give it a look. Most people ignored her or scowled and went wide.

That's when he realized she had to be the next one.

She was perfect. Someone no one would miss. She was virtually invisible to these bastards. Even as they were forced to walk around her, they still didn't seem to notice her. No one cared to stop and see what it was that she protecting, what she found that was so precious and fascinating that she insisted they walk around it.

And suddenly he couldn't wait. He wanted to cut her right now. Right here in the freezing cold sunny daylight. Right in the middle of the crowd that couldn't see her.

Except he hadn't brought his knife.

And so, he'd wait until tonight though his fingers fidgeted with anticipation.

He walked toward her. She was bent over now, touching the object. He decided it he couldn't resist. He needed to walk close enough just to see what it was. Then he'd be content to go back to his hotel suite and wait. He already knew where he could find her.

As he got closer he saw her wrapping her ragged knit gloves around the object that had captured her attention and sent her into such a protective mode. What in the world could have captured her attention? Someone's wallet? No, there was a sparkle. Cradled in her hands the sunlight glinted off of it. Perhaps someone's lost jewelry?

He was slowed down as he approached. A couple more steps and he was able to see her precious keepsake. The object was a long icicle. Dozens of others hung above from the awning that stretched halfway over the sidewalk. An icicle. *A frickin' icicle.*

He smiled to himself as he passed by and glanced at her. Her eyes flitted up to meet his and he wanted to tell her that he'd see her later. That it would be his pleasure to watch the surprise in those same eyes as her life spilled out of her.

Chapter 7

4:57 pm
Downtown Omaha

It was already getting dark by the time Maggie and Detective Pakula started walking the streets. There were crowds gathered at the ice rink and around the outside mall that stretched several city blocks long. Tonight was the lighting ceremony when hundreds of thousands of lights in trees and bushes and along rooftops would be turned on, marking the beginning of the holiday season.

"We've pulled in everybody on this, looking and talking to people since five this morning," he told her as they strolled the cobblestone streets, looking more like an old married couple than a couple of cops.

Pakula wore an old camouflage parka but nothing on his shaved head. Maggie kept on her leather jacket and added a red Huskers ballcap that Pakula had given her.

"It'll help you fit in," he told her about the cap.

She didn't argue. She was getting restless. Exhaustion had given way to the adrenaline that had taken over. Too much time had passed. Why did she ever believe they'd find this guy? It was like looking for a needle in a haystack.

She and Nick had wasted two whole hours pouring over

the security tapes only to come up empty handed. At one point they saw Gino enter the frame. According to Nick it looked like he was headed around the corner to the front door where he always came to meet Pete, the Rockwood Building's night security guard.

But then Gino stopped and turned as if someone had called to him. The camera didn't record sound. They watched Gino cock his head. He grinned and said something before walking back in the direction of who-ever had stopped him. He disappeared from the frame. Maggie didn't say it but she knew Gino had most likely headed right over to his killer.

Nick was taking this man's death personally and she didn't quite understand. Maybe it was because it happened outside one of his buildings. He had wanted to come with her and Pakula but they stopped him. He told them he had a license to carry. Pakula told him to go get his hand looked at.

"You should have had stitches," the detective told him, pointing to the wrapped hand that Maggie had noticed immediately but stopped herself from asking about. "You already bloodied up one of my crime scenes."

Pakula bought a hot chocolate for Maggie and a coffee for himself. The steam felt good on her frozen cheeks. She wrapped her hands around the cardboard cup and let it warm her fingers. She only had thin knit gloves. Why did she always come to this part of the country unprepared for the weather?

"You two married?" An old woman came up from behind them. She was trying to push a shopping cart filled with an odd assortment of junk.

"No, we're not married to each other." Pakula answered. "How are you doing? Do you have someplace warm to stay tonight?"

The woman didn't look like she heard him. Instead she muttered something to herself. She struggled to hike the cart over the curb that was still snow covered. Pakula grabbed the front end and lifted it easily onto the sidewalk for her.

"They've got some extra beds over at Saint Gabriel's," he tried again.

This time she blew out a raspberry at him. "I don't need no Saint Gabriel. Lydia and I have been taking care of each other for years."

Both Pakula and Maggie looked around at the same time, looking for someone named Lydia. There was obviously no one with this woman. People went around them, even stepping into the street to do so.

"Do you need me to help you find Lydia?" Pakula asked.

This time the woman stared directly into his eyes, her brow creasing under her dirty gray cap. She looked from him to Maggie then back at Pakula.

"You a cop?" she whispered.

Pakula was good but Maggie heard him clear his throat to cover his surprise.

"It's okay," the old woman reassured him, her face softening. She reached up and touched his arm, almost a grandmotherly gesture. "We've all heard about Gino." She shook her head. "A damned shame." Then she straightened and waved her hand like she was swatting at a fly. "Oh stop it, Lydia. You know who Gino was."

Pakula looked over at Maggie and raised his eyebrows.

The woman probably shouldn't be left on the streets. She obviously needed help but Maggie liked her feistiness and her spirit. As long as she had the shopping cart she was probably safe from their killer. He'd never be able to bump and slice her without having the click-clanking of that shopping cart in the way. It would draw too much attention.

Pakula was pulling out what looked like a business card. He handed it to the old woman.

"You know Danny at the coffee shop on the corner?"

Another raspberry but she took the card. "My God, who doesn't know Danny. That son of a bitch will talk your damned ear off. I take the coffee he gives me just to shut him up."

"You need anything," Pakula insisted, "You hand Danny that card and have him call me."

"What would I need? Me and Lydia we got everything we need right here." She tapped the shopping cart and the contents clanked and shifted.

They watched her rat-tat-tat down the street.

Maggie shook her head when Pakula glanced over at her.

"You can't lock them up," she told him. Though it would be easier to protect them if they were behind bars.

They started walking again. Past Vivace's and the aroma of garlic and warm bread made Maggie's stomach groan. She tried to remember the last time she had eaten. A doughnut that morning in the rental car. No wonder she was running low on energy. She sipped the rest of her hot chocolate.

"And there's another sorry ass," Pakula pointed to the homeless man in the ragged long black coat at the corner. "What am I going to do with these people?"

But as the man turned, both she and Pakula recognized him at the same time.

"What the hell are you doing here?" It was Maggie who posed the question.

Nick Morrelli spun around to face them. With a five o'clock shadow and a torn felt hat with the brim pulled down he looked like a street performer instead of the homeless man he thought he was portraying.

He simply shrugged at her and said, "You're not the boss of me." Then he jumped out into the street causing cars to brake and honk. He ran down the other sidewalk without looking back.

Chapter 8

6:15 pm
The Old Market

He had the knife with him, the cold metal tucked up into his sleeve.

The old woman had the cart with her again.

Damn! But she was so cute. Pulling crap like that on him.

In weeks past it would have made him angry, but his confidence was soaring again. And it didn't matter. He had ruled her out in just the last hour. He had a new target.

The guy reminded him of himself. A pathetic shadow of himself. That long dirty black coat that once upon a time was probably his power coat. Good looking guy, young. In good physical shape. Or at least he had been. Maybe he had been on the fast-track to success. Not anymore. Somewhere along the line he had stumbled big-time.

He followed the guy for a while and knew the man was plastered or flying high. He'd listened to him talk to several people. He made less sense than the old woman with her imaginary friend. No, this guy would probably be thanking him for doing him the service of putting him out of his misery.

Even earlier when the married couple had stopped the

guy. They seemed to recognize him. Or thought they did. The man danced around. Slung out some curses. Then he ran off, almost getting run over in the street. He was hilarious. A total loser. Nobody would miss this fool.

He watched him. Studied him. The streets were filling up with people. On one corner there was a four-piece band, or rather four teenagers with instruments, clanging out their version of Christmas songs. Horse-drawn carriages were keeping busy, too. Police horse patrol was back. Same as last night. The lighting ceremony had taken place about fifteen minutes ago and everywhere he looked he was bedazzled by tiny, twinkling white lights.

It was frickin' beautiful. What a lovely night to die.

He stepped out of a doorwell and found his target leaning against a rail, his back to an alley.

He'd have to do him from behind. Not a problem. He knew where to insert the blade. Not in the middle. It'd ram against the spinal cord. It would need to be off to the side. Down below. He'd keep the same angle up. The back tissue would require more pressure but the blade was long enough. He'd still puncture the heart. The only thing he'd miss was meeting the guy's eyes. Seeing the realization there.

Oh well. Sometimes he had to change up a little.

He headed in the other direction where he knew he could go around and up that alley. Soon, buddy. I'll take you out of your misery.

Chapter 9

6:18 pm

Pakula had to leave Maggie after a phone call from one of his officers. He thought he may have found the Night Slicer. A desk clerk at the Embassy Suites claimed she recognized the driver's license photo when the officer showed it to her. She said it looked a lot like the guy she checked in on Thursday.

She remembered him because she had complained about her bursitis and he gave her instructions of how long to keep a heating pad on it followed by ice. His remedy really worked and she was pretty sure he must be some kind of doctor. According to the clerk, he was booked through tomorrow morning. The officer was waiting for Pakula before they paid him a visit.

Pakula promised to call her. She wanted to be there if this was their guy. But it seemed too easy. Was it possible he'd be sitting in a hotel suite within ten blocks of where he'd killed Gino?

Maggie decided to backtrack and see if she could find Nick and talk some sense into him. She saw the old woman with her shopping cart set aside. The woman was staring at something in the snow along the side of a building. She seemed fixated on it even to the point of shooing people to take a wide circle around.

Then Maggie saw Nick.

He sat on a rail that in warmer weather probably allowed bike riders to chain up their bikes. His feet dangled. His head wobbled to the music from the street corner behind him. Sometimes the foot traffic got too close and brushed against him, sending his whole body teetering. No one seemed to notice him. Even when they jostled him or bumped him. He was playing his role very well.

She knew if she waved at him he'd ignore her. So instead, she started to walk toward him, walking against a crowd. She weaved her way through, taking her time and putting up with the occasion bump.

This is how he does it, she thought. And suddenly she knew he was here. She could feel him. Gut instinct. It had never failed her.

She looked at the faces coming toward her. Her arms came up across her chest and she walked like she was chilled and not paranoid that a knife would find its way into her chest. The flow of the crowd continued. She found herself pushed along the wall. And suddenly she felt a stab in her back. She spun around. But it was an elbow, not a knife.

Paranoid. She needed to stop.

Through a hole in the crowd she could see Nick, smiling, singing with the music. He was still sitting on the rail. Only now she saw a man coming out of the alley behind him. Well dressed. Alone. White ballcap. Focused on Nick. Walking directly toward Nick. His right arm down at his side.

Oh, God, she could see the flash of metal.

She started pushing her way through the crowd.

"Nick, behind you."

But her voice got drowned out in the noises of the street, the music, the crowd, the traffic. She shoved at bodies. Got shoved back a couple of times.

"FBI," she yelled but nobody moved out of the way for

the crazy woman in the red Huskers ballcap.

She tore at her jacket's zipper and yanked at her revolver. Ripped at the clasp to her shoulder holster.

Damn it!

The man was within three feet of Nick.

She waved her arms at him and finally he saw her. He waved back. Smiled. Then he tumbled forward, face down into the snow with the man falling on top of him. Even before she got there she could see the snow turning red.

"Oh God, no."

Then she saw the old woman. She pointed to the stiletto knife still clutched in the dead man's hand.

"That's the bastard that killed Gino," was all she said.

That's when Maggie saw the wide end of an icicle sticking out of the man's back.

Chapter 10

10:00 a.m.
Monday, December 5
Embassy Suites

Maggie had gotten five hours of sleep. For once she felt more than rested. She pulled on a pair of jeans and a favorite warm, bulky sweater and headed down to the lobby. Pakula already had a table. She saw him through the glass elevator. The same elevator John Robert Gunderson aka the Night Slicer had used for the last four days.

"I ordered our coffee," Pakula said, standing when she came to the table and pointing to the can of Diet Pepsi in Maggie's spot. She was impressed that he remembered her wake-up drink.

He had file folders piled up but pushed to the side of the table. She added one to his stack, information Tully had faxed to her late last night.

"So is Gunderson even his real name?" Pakula wanted to know.

"Yes."

They had found a small case inside his hotel suite that contained about a dozen driver's licenses and credit cards with various aliases. All the same initials. He's a traveling salesman," she said, taking a sip of the Diet Pepsi. "One of Bosco Blades top salesmen."

"Blades." Pakula shook his head. "Unbelievable."

"He flunked out of med school. I suspected he might have a medical background. He knew too much about where to stab. I just talked to Lieutenant Taylor Jackson this morning. Turns out one of his victims was a classmate of his. Heath Stover. He killed him in Nashville. We think he probably didn't want anyone to know he'd flunked out.

"Also, we now know he was in Nashville for a medical conference. Was supposed to do a presentation but canceled. We think he ran into Stover at the conference. Didn't expect to meet up with anyone who knew him or knew his past. Detective Killian told me there was a medical convention going on in New Orleans when he killed his two victims there. Kansas City was a conference for surgeons. And in Omaha—"

"The sales conference at the Quest Center," Pakula said, making the connection. "For medical devices or something, right?"

She nodded.

"How could he get away with it? Wouldn't his co-workers suspect something?"

"He worked out of a home office. Had a secretary at Bosco that he communicated with by phone, text and email. He met with his boss once a month. And he made all his travel arrangements on his own, so he could be whoever he wanted to be when he was on the road."

"He looked like an ordinary guy," Pakula said. "Best disguise there is."

"What about the old woman? You're not going to press charges are you?"

"Hell no. She did us a favor. I did get her off the streets."

"How did you manage that?"

"I know a guy who handles security for about a dozen buildings in the downtown area. Seems he was able to find a nice little apartment for her in one of them."

Maggie smiled. Of course Nick Morrelli would want to

take good care of the woman who saved his life.

"And what about Lydia?" she asked.

"Yeah, Lydia will be there with her. It appears this building even takes cats."

No one realized until last night that the old woman had an old calico cat that she kept bundled up and warm in the shopping cart.

"I've got to head out," Pakula gathered up his file folders and Maggie stood to walk him out before she went back up to the room. "Sure you can't stay for a day or two? My wife makes some of the best kolaches you'll ever eat."

"Maybe next time."

He shook her hand then muttered, "Aw the hell with it," and gave her a hug.

Just as he got to the door, Nick Morrelli came in. The two men exchanged greetings and then Nick's eyes found her.

He was clean-shaven this morning and dressed in crisp trousers and a bright red ski jacket. She stood in the archway to the restaurant area where only a few tables were occupied at this time on a Monday morning. She waited for him, watched him stride across the lobby. Last night when she thought he had been stabbed she had such a mix of emotions. Nick had a way of doing that to her.

He wasn't relationship material, she reminded herself as he got closer and she couldn't pull her eyes away from his. He had called early this morning, asking if they could spend some time together. Maybe go ice-skating. Take a carriage ride. She had agreed. Now as she got a whiff of his aftershave she wondered if perhaps that wasn't such a wise decision.

He pointed to something over her head.

"You're always giving me mixed signals, Maggie O'Dell," he told her.

She looked up to see the mistletoe hanging high above her in the archway. Before she could say a word he was kissing her. And suddenly she found herself thinking *it might just be too cold to leave the hotel.*

MEET J.T. ELLISON

New York Times bestselling author **J.T. Ellison** writes dark psychological thrillers starring Nashville Homicide Lt. Taylor Jackson and medical examiner Dr. Samantha Owens, and pens the Nicholas Drummond series with #1 *New York Times* bestselling author Catherine Coulter. Co-host of the premier literary television show, *A Word on Words*, Ellison lives in Nashville with her husband and twin kittens.

For more insight into her wicked imagination, join J.T.'s email list at jtellison.com/subscribe, or follow her online at Facebook.com/JTEllison14 or on Twitter @thrillerchick.

MEET ALEX KAVA

Alex Kava is the *New York Times* and International bestselling author of the critically acclaimed Maggie O'Dell series and a new series featuring former Marine, Ryder Creed and his K-9 dogs

Her stand-alone novel, *One False Move*, was chosen for the 2006 One Book One Nebraska and her political thriller, *Whitewash*, was one of *January Magazine's* best thrillers of the year. Her novel, *Stranded* was awarded both a Florida Book Award and the Nebraska Book Award.

Published in over thirty-three countries, Alex's novels have made the bestseller lists in the UK, Australia, Germany, Japan, Italy and Poland.

She is currently working on BEFORE EVIL, a prequel to A Perfect Evil, and LOST CREED, the next in-line of the Creed series.

MEET ERICA SPINDLER

Erica Spindler is the *New York Times* and International Chart bestselling author of thirty-two novels and three eNovellas. Spindler's skill for crafting engrossing plots and compelling characters has earned both critical praise and legions of fans. Published across the globe, she's been called "The Master of Addictive Suspense" and "The Queen of the Romantic Thriller."

Her most recent novels are THE FINAL SEVEN and TRIPLE SIX, books one and two in her *The Lightkeepers* series.

Spindler splits her writing time between her New Orleans area home and a lakeside writing retreat. She's married to her college sweetheart, has two sons and the constant companionship of Roxie, *the wonder retriever*.

She is busy writing her next thriller, THE OTHER GIRL and FALLEN FIVE, book three in *The Lightkeepers*.

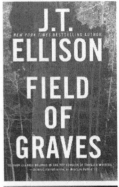

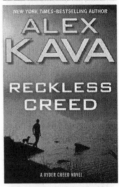

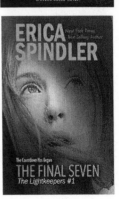

Turn the page
for excerpts from
their latest novels

Available from
Amazon,
Barnes & Noble
and Independent
Booksellers
thru
INDIEBOUND.org

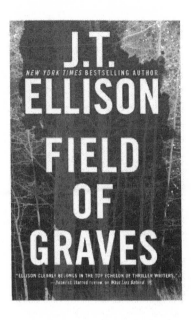

With FIELD OF GRAVES, *New York Times* bestselling author J.T. Ellison goes back to where it all began...

All of Nashville is on edge with a serial killer on the loose. A madman is trying to create his own end-of-days apocalypse and the cops trying to catch him are almost as damaged as the killer. Field of Graves reveals the origins of some of J.T. Ellison's most famous creations: the haunted Lieutenant Taylor Jackson; her blunt, exceptional best friend, medical examiner Dr. Samantha Owens; and troubled FBI profiler Dr. John Baldwin. Together, they race the clock and their own demons to find the killer before he claims yet another victim. This dark, thrilling and utterly compelling novel will have readers on the edge of their seats, and Ellison's fans will be delighted with the revelations about their favorite characters.

Prologue

Taylor picked up her portable phone for the tenth time in ten minutes. She hit Redial, heard the call connect and start ringing, then clicked the Off button and returned the phone to her lap. Once she made this call, there was no going back. Being right wouldn't make her the golden girl. If she were wrong—well, she didn't want to think about what could happen. Losing her job would be the least of her worries.

Damned if she did. Damned if she didn't.

She set the phone on the pool table and went down the stairs of her small two-story cabin. In the kitchen, she opened the door to the refrigerator and pulled out a Diet Coke. She laughed to herself. As if more caffeine would give her the courage to make the call. She should try a shot of whiskey. That always worked in the movies.

She snapped open the tab and stood staring out of her kitchen window. It had been dark for hours—the moon gone and the inky blackness outside her window impenetrable—but in an hour the skies would lighten. She would have to make a decision by then.

She turned away from the window and heard a loud crack. The lights went out. She jumped a mile, then giggled nervously, a hand to her chest to stop the sudden pounding.

121

Silly girl, she thought. *The lights go out all the time. There was a Nashville Electric Service crew on the corner when you drove in earlier; they must have messed up the line and a power surge caused the lights to blow. It happens every time NES works on the lines. Now stop it. You're a grown woman. You're not afraid of the dark.*

She reached into her junk drawer and groped for a flashlight. Thumbing the switch, she cursed softly when the light didn't shine. Batteries, where were the batteries?

She froze when she heard the noise and immediately went on alert, all of her senses going into overdrive. She strained her ears, trying to hear it again. Yes, there it was. A soft scrape off the back porch. She took a deep breath and sidled out of the kitchen, keeping close to the wall, moving lightly toward the back door. She brought her hand to her side and found nothing. Damn it. She'd left her gun upstairs.

The tinkling of breaking glass brought her up short.

The French doors leading into the backyard had been breached. It was too late to head upstairs and get the gun. She would have to walk right through the living room to get to the stairs. Whoever had just broken through her back door was not going to let her stroll on by. She started edging back toward the kitchen, holding her breath, as if that would help her not make any noise.

She didn't see the fist, only felt it crack against her jaw. Her eyes swelled with tears, and before she could react, the fist connected again. She spun and hit the wall face first. The impact knocked her breath out. Her lips cut on the edge of her teeth; she tasted blood. The intruder grabbed her as she started to slide down the wall. Yanked her to her feet and put his hands around her throat, squeezing hard.

Now she knew exactly where her attacker was, and she fought back with everything she had. She struggled against him, quickly realizing she was in trouble. He was stronger than her, bigger than her. And he was there to kill.

She went limp, lolled bonelessly against him, surprising

him with the sudden weight. He released one arm in response, and she took that moment to whirl around and shove with all her might. It created some space between them, enabling her to slip out of his grasp. She turned quickly but crashed into the slate end table. He was all over her. They struggled their way into the living room. She began to plan. Kicked away again.

Her attacker lunged after her. She used the sturdy side table to brace herself and whipped out her left arm in a perfect jab, aiming lower than where she suspected his chin would be. She connected perfectly and heard him grunt in pain. Spitting blood out of her mouth in satisfaction, she followed the punch with a kick to his stomach, heard the *whoosh* of his breath as it left his body. He fell hard against the wall. She spun away and leapt to the stairs. He jumped up to pursue her, but she was quicker. She pounded up the stairs as fast as she could, rounding the corner into the hall just as her attacker reached the landing. Her weapon was in its holster, on the bookshelf next to the pool table, right where she had left it when she'd gone downstairs for the soda. She was getting careless. She should never have taken it off her hip. With everything that was happening, she shouldn't have taken for granted that she was safe in her own home.

Her hand closed around the handle of the weapon. She pulled the Glock from its holster, whipped around to face the door as the man came tearing through it. She didn't stop to think about the repercussions, simply reacted. Her hand rose by instinct, and she put a bullet right between his eyes. His momentum carried him forward a few paces. He was only five feet from her, eyes black in death, when he dropped with a thud.

She heard her own ragged breathing. She tasted blood and raised a bruised hand to her jaw, feeling her lips and her teeth gingerly. Son of a bitch had caught her right in the jaw and loosened two molars. The adrenaline rush left her. She collapsed on the floor next to the lifeless body. She might have even slept for a moment.

The throbbing in her jaw brought her back. Morning was beginning to break, enough to see the horrible mess in front of her. The cat was sit-ting on the pool table, watching her curiously.

Rising, she took in the scene. The man was collapsed on her game room floor, slowly leaking blood on her Berber carpet. She peered at the stain.

That's going to be a bitch to get out.

She shook her head to clear the cobwebs. What an inane thing to say. Shock, she must be going into shock. How long had they fought? Had it been only five minutes? Half an hour? She felt as though she had struggled against him for days; her body was tired and sore. Never mind the blood caked around her mouth. She put her hand up to her face. Make that her nose too.

She eyed the man again. He was facedown and angled slightly to one side. She slipped her toes under his right arm and flipped him over with her foot. The shot was true; she could see a clean entry wound in his forehead. Reaching down out of habit, she felt for his carotid pulse, but there was nothing. He was definitely dead.

"Oh, David," she said. "You absolute idiot. Look what you've made me do."

Now the shit was absolutely going to hit the fan. It was time to make the call.

Chapter 1

Three months later
Nashville, Tennessee

Bodies, everywhere bodies, a field of graves, limbs and torsos and heads, all left above ground. The feeling of dirt in her mouth, grimy and thick; the whispers from the dead, long arms reaching for her as she passed through the carnage. Ghostly voices, soft and sibilant. "Help us. Why won't you help us?"

Taylor jerked awake, sweating, eyes wild and blind in the darkness. The sheets twisted around her body in a claustrophobic shroud, and she struggled to get them untangled. She squeezed her eyes shut, willed her breathing back to normal, trying to relax, to let the grisly images go. When she opened her eyes, the room was still dark but no longer menacing. Her screams had faded away into the silence. The cat jumped off the bed with a disgruntled meow in response to her thrashing.

She laid her head back on the pillow, swallowed hard, still unable to get a full breath.

Every damn night. She was starting to wonder if she'd ever sleep well again.

She wiped a hand across her face and looked at the clock:

6:10 a.m. The alarm was set for seven, but she wasn't going to get any more rest. She might as well get up and get ready for work. Go in a little early, see what horrors had captured the city overnight.

She rolled off the bed, trying hard to forget the dream. Showered, dressed, dragged on jeans and a black cashmere T-shirt under a black motorcycle jacket, stepped into her favorite boots. Put her creds in her pocket and her gun on her hip. Pulled her wet hair off her face and into a ponytail.

Time to face another day.

She was in her car when the call came. "Morning, Fitz. What's up?"

"Morning, LT. We have us a body at the Parthenon."

"I'll be right there."

* * * *

It might have become a perfect late autumn morning. The sky was busy, turning from white to blue as dawn rudely forced its way into day. Birds were returning from their mysterious nocturnal errands, greeting and chattering about the night's affairs. The air was clear and heavy, still muggy from the overnight heat but holding a hint of coolness, like an ice cube dropped into a steaming mug of coffee. The sky would soon shift to sapphire the way only autumn skies do, as clear and heavy as the precious stone itself.

The beauty of the morning was lost on Lieutenant Taylor Jackson, Criminal Investigation Division, Nashville Metro Police. She snapped her long body under the yellow crime scene tape and looked around for a moment. Sensed the looks from the officers around her. Straightened her shoulders and marched toward them.

Metro officers had been traipsing around the crime scene control area like it was a cocktail party, drinking coffee and chatting each other up as though they'd been apart for weeks, not hours. The grass was already littered with cups, cigarette butts, crumpled notebook paper, and at least one copy of the morning's sports section from *The Tennessean*. Taylor cursed silently; they knew better than this. One of these yahoos was going to inadvertently contaminate a crime scene one of these days, send in her team off on a wild goose chase. Guess whose ass would be in the proverbial sling then?

She stooped to grab the sports page, surreptitiously glanced at the headline regaling the Tennessee Titans' latest win, then crumpled it into a firm ball in her hands.

Taylor didn't know what information about the murder had leaked out over the air, but the curiosity factor had obviously kicked into high gear. An officer she recognized from another sector was cruising by to check things out, not wanting to miss out on all the fun. Media vans lined the street. Joggers pretending not to notice anything was happening nearly tripped trying to see what all the fuss was about. Exactly what she needed on no sleep: everyone willing to help, to get in and screw up her crime scene.

Striding toward the melee, she tried to tell herself that it wasn't their fault she'd been up all night. At least she'd had a shower and downed two Diet Cokes, or she would have arrested them all.

She reached the command post and pasted on a smile. "Mornin', kids. How many of you have dragged this crap through my crime scene?" She tossed the balled up paper at the closest officer.

She tried to keep her tone light, as if she were amused by their shenanigans, but she didn't fool anyone, and the levity disappeared from the gathering. The brass was on the scene, so all the fun had come to a screeching halt. Uniforms who didn't belong started to drift away, one or two giving Taylor a sideways glance. She ignored them, the way she ignored most things these days.

As a patrol officer, she'd kept her head down, worked her cases, and developed a reputation for being a straight shooter. Her dedication and clean work had been rewarded with promotion after promotion; she was in plainclothes at twenty-eight. She'd caught a nasty first case in Homicide—the kidnapping and murder of a young girl. She'd nailed the bastard who'd done it; Richard Curtis was on death row now. The case made the national news and sent her career into overdrive. She quickly became known for being a hard-hitting investigator and moved up the ranks from detective to lead to sergeant, until she'd been given the plum job she had now—homicide lieutenant.

If her promotion to lieutenant at the tender age of thirty-four had rankled some of the more traditional officers on the force, the death of David Martin—one of their own—made it ten times worse. There were always going to be cops who tried to make her life difficult; it was part of being a chick on the force, part of having a reputation. Taylor was tough, smart, and liked to do things her own way to get the job done. The majority of the men she worked with had great respect for her abilities. There were always going to be detractors, cops who whispered behind her back, but in Taylor's mind, success trumped rumor every time.

Then Martin had decided to ruin her life and nearly derailed her career in the process. She was still clawing her way back.

Taylor's second in command, Detective Pete Fitzgerald, lumbered toward her, the ever-present unlit cigarette hanging out of his mouth. He'd quit a couple of years before, after a minor heart attack, but kept one around to light in case of an emergency. Fitz had an impressive paunch; his belly reached Taylor before the rest of his body.

"Hey, LT. Sorry I had to drag you away from your beauty sleep." He looked her over, concern dawning in his eyes. "I was just kidding. What's up with you? You look like shit warmed over."

Taylor waved a hand in dismissal. "Didn't sleep. Aren't we supposed to have some sort of eclipse this morning? I think it's got me all out of whack."

Fitz took the hint and backed down. "Yeah, we are." He looked up quickly, shielding his eyes with his hand. "See, it's already started."

He was right. The moon was moving quickly across the sun, the crime scene darkening by the minute. "Eerie," she said.

He looked back at her, blinking hard. "No kidding. Remind me not to stare into the sun again."

"Will do. Celestial phenomenon aside, what do we have here?"

"Okay, darlin', here we go. We have a couple of lovebirds who decided to take an early morning stroll—found themselves a deceased Caucasian female on the Parthenon's steps. She's sitting up there pretty as you please, just leaning against the gate in front of the Parthenon doors like she sat down for a rest. Naked as a jaybird too, and very, very dead."

Taylor turned her gaze to the Parthenon. One of her favorite sites in Nashville, smack-dab in the middle of Centennial Park, the full-size replica was a huge draw for tourists and classicists alike. The statue of Athena inside was awe-inspiring. She couldn't count how many school field trips she'd been on here over the years. Leaving a body on the steps was one hell of a statement.

"Where are the witnesses?"

"Got the lovebirds separated, but the woman's having fits—we haven't been able to get a full statement. The scene's taped off. Traffic on West End has been blocked off, and we've closed all roads into and around Centennial Park. ME and her team have been here about fifteen minutes. Oh, and our killer was here at some point too." He grinned at her lopsidedly. "He dumped her sometime overnight, only the duckies and geese in the lake saw him. This is gonna be a bitch to canvass. Do you think we can admit 'AFLAC' as a statement in court?"

Taylor gave him a quick look and a perfunctory laugh, more amused at imagining Fitz waddling about like the duck from the insurance ads quacking than at his irreverent attitude. She knew better, but it did seem as if he was having a good time. Taylor understood that sometimes inappropriate attempts at humor were the only way a cop could make it through the day, so she chastised him gently. "You've got a sick sense of humor, Fitz." She sighed, turning off all personal thoughts, becoming a cop again. All business, all the time. That's what they needed to see from her.

"We'll probably have to go public and ask who was here last night and when, but I'm not holding my breath that we'll get anything helpful, so let's put it off for now."

He nodded in agreement. "Do you want to put up the chopper? Probably useless—whoever dumped her is long gone."

"I think you're right." She jerked her head toward the Parthenon steps. "What's he trying to tell us?"

Fitz looked toward the doors of the Parthenon, where the medical examiner was crouched over the naked body. His voice dropped, and he suddenly became serious. "I don't know, but this is going to get ugly, Taylor. I got a bad feeling."

Taylor held a hand up to cut him off. "C'mon, man, they're all ugly. It's too early to start spinning. Let's just get through the morning. Keep the frickin' media out of here—put 'em down in the duck shit if you have to. You can let them know which roads are closed so they can get the word out to their traffic helicopters, but that's it. Make sure the uniforms keep everyone off the tape. I don't want another soul in here until I have a chance to be fully briefed by all involved. Has the Park Police captain shown up yet?"

Fitz shook his head. "Nah. They've called him, but I haven't seen him."

"Well, find him, too. Make sure they know which end is up. Let's get the perimeter of this park searched, grid by grid, see if we find something. Get K-9 out here, let them do an article search. Since the roads are already shut off, tell them to expand the perimeter one thousand outside the borders of the park. I want to see them crawling around like ants at a picnic. I see any of them hanging in McDonald's before this is done, I'm kicking some butt."

Fitz gave her a mock salute. "I'm on it. When Sam determined she was dumped, I went ahead and called K-9, and pulled all the officers coming off duty. We may have an overtime situation, but I figured with your, um, finesse..." He snorted out the last word, and Taylor eyed him coolly.

"I'll handle it." She pushed her hair back from her face and reestablished her hurried ponytail. "Get them ready for all hell to break loose. I'm gonna go talk to Sam."

"Glad to serve, love. Now go see Sam, and let the rest of us grunts do our jobs. If you decide you want the whirlybird, give me a thumbs-up." He blew her a kiss and marched toward the command post, snapping his fingers at the officers to get their attention.

Turning toward the building, she caught a stare from one of the older patrols. His gaze was hostile, lip curled in a sneer. She gave him her most brilliant smile, making his scowl deepen. She broke off the look, shaking her head. She didn't have time to worry about politics right now.

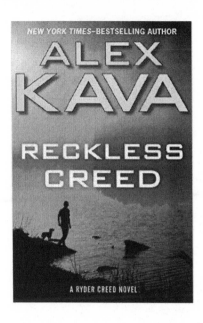

In the new edge-of-your-seat thriller from *New York Times* bestselling author Alex Kava, Ryder Creed, his K-9 search-and-rescue dogs, and FBI agent Maggie O'Dell find themselves at the center of a dire and mysterious case.

In Chicago, a young man jumps from his thirtieth-story hotel room; along the Missouri river, a hunter and his son stumble upon a lake whose surface is littered with snow geese, all of them dead; and in southern Alabama, Ryder Creed and his search-and-rescue dog Grace find the body of a young woman who went missing in the Conecuh National Forest...and it appears she filled her pockets with rocks and walked into the river. Before long Ryder Creed and FBI profiler Maggie O'Dell will discover the ominous connection among these mysterious deaths. What they find may be the most prolific killer the United States has ever known.

BONUS MATERIAL

134

Chapter 1

Chicago

Tony Briggs coughed up blood, then wiped his mouth with his shirt-sleeve. This was bad. Although it was nothing he couldn't handle. He'd been through worse. Lots worse. But still, they didn't tell him he'd get this sick. He was beginning to think the bastards had double-crossed him.

He tapped out, "fine mess I got myself into," on his cell phone and hit SEND before he changed his mind.

The text message wasn't part of his instructions. Not part of the deal. He didn't care. So what if the watchers found out. What could they do to him now? He already felt like crap. They couldn't make him feel much worse.

He tossed the phone into the garbage can along with the few brochures he'd picked up throughout the day. His itinerary read like a sight-seeing family vacation. Or in his case, something presented by one of those make-a-wish charities – one final trip, all expenses paid.

He laughed at that and ended up in a coughing fit. Blood sprayed the flat screen TV and even the wall behind. He didn't like leaving the mess for the hotel housekeeping staff. But it was a little too late for that. Especially since his instructions included touching everything he could throughout the day. The list rattled in his head: light switches, elevator buttons, restaurant menus, remote control, and escalator handrails.

Earlier that morning at the McDonald's—before the cough, just before the fever spiked and he still had a bit of bravado along with an appetite—he felt his first tinge of apprehension. He'd taken his tray and stopped at the condiment counter.

Touch as many surfaces as possible.

That's what he'd been told. Germs could live on a hard surface for up to eighteen hours. He may have screwed up a lot of things in his life but he could still follow instructions.

That's what he'd been thinking when he felt a tap on his elbow.

"Hey, mister, could you please hand me two straws?"

The kid was six, maybe seven with nerdy glasses, the thick black frames way too big for his face. He kept shoving at them, the motion second nature. The kid reminded Tony immediately of his best friend, Jason. They had grown up together since they were six years old. Same schools. Same football team. Joined the Army together. Even came back from Afghanistan, both screwed up in one way or another. Tony was the athlete. Jason was the brains. Smart and pushy even at six. But always following Tony around.

Old four eyes.

"Whadya doing now?" was Jason's favorite catch phrase.

In grade school they went through a period where Jason mimicked everything Tony did. In high school the kid bulked up just so he could be on the football team, right alongside Tony. In the back of his mind he knew Jason probably joined the Army only because Tony wanted to. And look where it got them.

Tony shoved at the guilt. And suddenly at that moment he found himself hoping that Jason never found out what a coward he really was.

"Mister," the kid waited with his hand outstretched.

Tony caught himself reaching for the damned straw dispenser then stopped short, fingertips inches away.

"Get your own damned straws," he told the kid. "You're not crippled."

Then he turned and left without even getting his own straw or napkin. Without touching a single thing on the whole frickin' condiment counter. In fact, he took his tray and walked out, shouldering the door open so he wouldn't have to touch it either. He dumped the tray and food in a nearby trashcan. The kid had unnerved him so much it took him almost an hour to move on.

Now back in his hotel room, sweat trickled down his face. He wiped at his forehead with the same sleeve he'd used on his mouth.

The fever was something he'd expected. The blurred vision was a surprise.

No, it was more than blurred vision. The last hour or so he knew he'd been having hallucinations. He thought he saw one of his old drill sergeants in the lobby of the John Hancock building. But he'd been too nauseated from the observatory to check it out. Still, he remembered to touch every single button before he got out of the elevator. Nauseated and weak-kneed.

And he was embarrassed.

His mind might not be what it once was thanks to what the doctors called traumatic brain injury, but he was proud that he'd kept his body lean and strong when so many of his buddies had come back without limbs. Now the muscle fatigue set in and it actually hurt to breathe.

Just then Tony heard a click in the hotel room. It came from somewhere behind him. It sounded like the door.

The room's entrance had a small alcove for the minibar and coffee maker. He couldn't see the door without crossing the room.

"Is anybody there?" he asked as he stood up out of the chair.

Was he hallucinating again or had a shadow moved?

Suddenly everything swirled and tipped to the right. He leaned against the room service cart. He'd ordered it just like his watchers had instructed him to do when he got back to his room. Nevermind that he hadn't been able to eat a thing. Even the scent of fresh strawberries made his stomach roil.

No one was there.

Maybe the fever was making him paranoid. It certainly made him feel like he was burning up from the inside. He needed to cool down. Get some fresh air.

Tony opened the patio door and immediately shivered. The small cement balcony had a cast-iron railing, probably one of the original fixtures that the hotel decided to keep when renovating—something quaint and historic.

The air felt good. Cold against his sweat-drenched body, but good. Made him feel alive. And he smiled at that. Funny how being this sick could make him feel so alive. He'd come close to being killed in Afghanistan several times, knew the exhilaration afterwards.

He stepped out into the night. His head was still three pounds too heavy, but the swirling sensation had eased a bit. And he could breathe finally without hacking up blood.

Listening to the rumble and buzz of the city below he realized if he wanted to, there'd be nothing to this. He had contemplated his own death many times since coming home but never once had he imagined this.

Suddenly he realized it'd be just like stepping out of a C-130.

Only without a parachute.

Nineteen stories made everything look like a miniature world below. Matchbox cars. The kind he and Jason had played with. Fought over. Traded. Shared.

And that's when his second wave of nausea hit him.

Maybe he didn't have to finish this. He didn't even care any more whether they paid him or not. Maybe it wasn't too late to get to an emergency room. They could probably give him something. Then he'd just go home. There were easier ways to make a few bucks.

But as he started to turn around he felt a shove. Not the wind. Strong hands. A shadow. His arms flailed trying to restore his balance.

Another shove.

His fingers grabbed for the railing but his body was already tipping. The metal dug into the small of his back. His vision blurred with streaks of light. His ears filled with the echo of a wind tunnel. The cold air surrounded him.

No second chances. He was already falling.

Chapter 2

Conecuh National Forest
Just north of the Alabama/Florida state line

Ryder Creed's T-shirt stuck to his back. His hiking boots felt like cement blocks, caked with red clay. The air grew heavier, wet and stifling. The scent of pine mixed with the gamy smell of exertion from both man and dog. This deep in the woods even the birds were different, the drilling of the red-cockaded woodpecker the only sound to interrupt the continuous buzz of mosquitoes.

He was grateful for the long-sleeved shirt and the kerchief around his neck as well as the one around Grace's. The fabric had been soaked in a special concoction that his business partner, Hannah, had mixed up, guaranteed to repel bugs. Hannah joked that one more ingredient and maybe it'd even keep them safe from vampires.

In a few hours it would be nighttime in the forest, and deep in the sticks, as they called it, on the border of Alabama and Florida, there were enough reasons to drive a man to believe in vampires. The kudzu climbed and twisted up the trees so thick it looked like green netting. There were places the sunlight couldn't squeeze down through the branches.

Their original path was quickly becoming overgrown. Thorny vines grabbed at Creed's pantlegs, and he worried they were ripping into Grace's short legs. He was already second-guessing bringing the Jack Russell terrier instead of one of his bigger dogs, but Grace was the best air scent dog he had in a pack of dozens. And she was scampering along en-joying the adventure, making her way easily through the tall longleaf pines that grew so close Creed had to sidestep in spots.

They had less than an hour until sunset, and yet the federal agent from Atlanta was still questioning Creed.

"You don't think you need more than the one dog?"

Agent Lawrence Taber had already remarked several times about how small Grace was, and that she was "kind of scrawny." Creed heard him whisper to Sheriff Wylie that he was "pretty sure Labs or German shepherds were the best trackers."

Creed was used to it. He knew that neither he nor his dogs were what most law enforcement officers expected. He'd been training and handling dogs for over seven years. His business, K9 CrimeScents, had a waiting list for his dogs. Yet people expected him to be older, and his dogs to be bigger.

Grace was actually one of his smallest dogs, a scrappy brown-and-white Jack Russell terrier. Creed had discovered her abandoned at the end of his long driveway. When he found her she was skin and bones but sagging where she had recently been nursing puppies. Locals had gotten into the habit of leaving their unwanted dogs at the end of Creed's fifty-acre property. It wasn't the first time he had seen a female dog dumped and punished when the owner was simply too cheap to get her spayed.

Hannah didn't like that people took advantage of Creed's soft heart. But what no one—not even Hannah—understood was that the dogs Creed rescued were some of his best air scent trackers. Skill was only a part of the training. Bonding with the trainer was another. His rescued dogs trusted him unconditionally and were loyal beyond measure. They were eager to learn and anxious to please. And Grace was one of his best.

"Working multiple dogs at the same time can present problems," he finally told the agent. "Competition between the dogs. False alerts. Over-lapping grids. Believe me, one dog will be more than sufficient."

Creed kept his tone matter of fact for Grace's sake. Emotion runs down the leash. Dogs could detect their handler's mood, so Creed always tried to keep his temper in check even when guys like Agent Taber started to piss him off.

He couldn't help wonder why Tabor was here, but he kept it to himself. Creed wasn't law enforcement. He was hired to do a job and had no interest in questioning jurisdiction or getting involved in the pissing contests that local and federal officials often got into.

"I can't think she'd run off this far," Sheriff Wylie said.

He was talking about the young woman they were looking for. The reason they were out here searching. But now Creed realized the sheriff was starting to question his judgment, too, even though the two of them had worked together plenty of times.

Creed ignored both men as best he could and concentrated on Grace. He could hear her breathing getting more rapid. She started to hold her nose higher and he tightened his grip on the leash. She had definitely entered a scent cone but Creed had no idea if it was secondary or primary. All he could smell was the river, but that wasn't what had Grace's attention.

"How long has she been gone?" Creed asked Sheriff Wylie.

"Since the night before last."

Creed had been told that Izzy Donner was nineteen, a recovering drug addict who was getting her life back on track. She had enrolled in college part-time and was even looking forward to a trip to Atlanta she had planned with friends. Creed still wasn't quite sure why her family had panicked. A couple nights out of touch didn't seem out of ordinary for a teenager.

"Tell me again why you think she ran off into the forest. Are you sure she wasn't taken against her will?"

Seemed like a logical reason that a federal agent might be involved if the girl had been taken. The two men exchanged a glance. Creed suspected they were withholding information from him.

"Why would it matter?" Tabor finally asked. "If your dog is any good it should still be able to find her, right?"

"It would matter because there'd be another person's scent."

"We had a tip called in," Wylie admitted but Tabor shot him a look and cut him off from saying anything else.

Before Creed could push for more, Grace started straining at the end of the leash. Her breathing had increased, her nose and whiskers twitched. He knew she was headed for the river.

"Slow down a bit, Grace," he told her.

Slow down was something a handler didn't like telling his dog. But sometimes the drive could take over and send a dog barreling through dangerous terrain. He'd heard of working dogs scraping their pads raw, so focused and excited about finding the scent that would reward them.

Grace kept pulling. Creed's long legs were moving fast to keep up. The tangle of vines threatened to trip him while Grace skipped between them, jumping over fallen branches and straining at the end of her leash. He focused on keeping up with her and not letting go.

Only now did Creed notice that Agent Tabor and Sheriff Wylie were trailing farther behind. He didn't glance back but could hear their voices becoming more muffled, interspersed with some curses as they tried to navigate the prickly underbrush.

Finally Grace slowed down. Then she stopped. But the

little dog was still frantically sniffing the air. Creed could see and hear the river five feet away. He watched Grace and waited. Suddenly the dog looked up to find his eyes and stared at him.

This was their signal. Creed knew the dog wasn't trying to determine what direction to go next, nor was she looking to him for instructions. Grace was telling him she had found their target. That she knew exactly where it was but she didn't want to go any closer.

Something was wrong.

"What is it?" Sheriff Wylie asked while he and Tabor approached, trying to catch their breaths and keep a safe distance.

"I think she's in the water," Creed said.

"What do you mean she's in the water," Tabor asked.

But Wylie understood. "Oh crap."

"Grace, stay," Creed told the dog and dropped the leash.

He knew he didn't need the command. The dog was spooked and it made Creed's stomach start to knot up.

He maneuvered his way over the muddy clay of the riverbank, hold-in onto tree branches to keep from sliding. He didn't know that Wylie was close behind until he heard the older man's breath catch at the same time that Creed saw the girl's body.

Her eyes stared up as if she were watching the clouds. The girl's windbreaker was still zipped up and had ballooned out, causing her up-per body to float while the rest of her lay on the sandy bottom. This part of Blackwater River was only about three feet deep. Though tea-colored, the water was clear. And even in the fading sunlight Creed could see that the girl's pockets were weighted down.

"Son of bitch," he heard Wylie say from behind. "Looks like she loaded up her pockets with rocks and walked right into the river."

Detectives Micki Dare and Zach Harris are back in TRIPLE SIX, their second adventure in Erica Spindler's supernatural thriller series The Lightkeepers.

It's been three months since that night - the night that Micki almost died. Physically, she's healed but the nightmares remain, and she can't shake the feeling that more happened that night than Zach is telling her. The only thing she can do is try to carry on as normal and solve the latest case she and Zach have been assigned to.

A string of brutal home invasions are rocking New Orleans and the families targeted seemingly have nothing in common. Why were these victims chosen? The deeper Micki and Zach go into the case, the more they realize something isn't right. There's something familiar about the person doing this - and it's a familiarity Micki has been trying to forget. Suddenly, this case is hitting too close to home and Micki has to decide if she really wants to learn the truth about that night . . .

Prologue

New Orleans, Louisiana
Monday, July 22nd
3:00 p.m.

Lost Angel Ministries. Zach Harris stood at the wrought iron gate, gazing at the sign as it swayed in the breeze. The iron fence circled the property, a Victorian home from days gone by, repurposed into a center that helped lost and disenfranchised youth. Youth who were special. Very. The front door opened and a teenager darted out, calling 'bye over her shoulder. She was small with a spiky, pixie haircut, the spikes dyed Irish green. She met his eyes as she reached the gate. Beautiful eyes. A brilliant green that matched her hair.

She was one of them. Lightkeeper.

Or like him, a mutation of one.

"Hey," she said, slipping past him.

"Hey," he responded back, and headed through the gate and up the walk. It felt weird, thinking of himself that way. A light being enrobed in human flesh? Sent to guide the human race, steer it toward good. Mortal angels in a life or death battle with an ancient evil?

147

It felt like total bullshit. It pissed him off. He might not want to buy in, but at this point, he didn't have a choice. Like it or not, his eyes had been opened.

From the neutral ground behind him came the rumble of the streetcar. He glanced over his shoulder at it, bright, shiny red, windows shut tight to keep the heat out. He reached the door, looked directly at the security camera and was buzzed in.

Eli met him in the foyer. He looked no worse for wear, as if saving lives and battling the forces of darkness had the rejuvenating properties of a spa day.

"Zach, buddy—" He clapped him on the back. "—great to see you. Come, they're in the conference room."

They started in that direction. Eli turned his extraordinary gaze on him. "You've been to the hospital and seen Michaela?"

"Left just a little bit ago."

"How is she?"

"Healing quickly. Very."

"I do good work."

The cockiness annoyed the crap out of him. "She says she remembers being surrounded by a beautiful, healing light. Like being wrapped in an angel's wings."

Eli stopped and cocked his head. "Did she? That's curious. And what did you tell her?"

"That she had lost a lot of blood, was in shock or hallucinating."

"Good. Here we are."

"Wait." Zach laid a hand on his arm, stopping him. "I thought you said she wouldn't remember anything."

"That's why it's curious." He smiled. "I don't think it's anything you need to worry about."

Famous last words, Zach thought and stepped into the conference room. Only two at the table: Parker and Professor Truebell.

"Zachary." Truebell stood and held out his hand, smiling.

148

Zach took it. "Professor."

"No worse for wear, I see."

"Tell that to every muscle, joint and bone in my body." He indicated the four of them. "We're it?"

"For today, yes."

"No Angel?"

"She's not ready."

The comment rankled. More secrets. More need-to-know bullshit. "I see nothing's changed since the last time I sat across this table from you."

The elfin Truebell shook his head. "Everything's changed, Zachary. Sit. Please."

He did. Parker spoke up. "No hello for me, Zach?"

He looked at him, not masking his anger. "I may have to work with you, Special Agent Parker, but I don't have to like you. And I sure as hell don't have to respect you."

Parker leaned back in his chair and folded his arms across his chest. "You don't think that's a little harsh? And formal, considering we're family?"

"You lied to me. Manipulated me. You kept your real identity a secret from me." He arched his eyebrows. "No. Not too harsh. And as for the last part, I don't have anyone's word on that but yours."

"You'll come around."

"Don't count on it." He shifted his attention back to Truebell. "Why am I here today?"

"You know why."

"Do I?"

"Are you in," Truebell asked, "or out?"

He wished he could say he was out, shake this whole experience off, and go back to the life he had known before. But that life was gone forever. "Saturday made a believer out of me."

He nodded. "You know it's destructive power now. You understand our urgency."

His head filled with the memory of that power turned on

149

him, his helplessness against it. "Yes."

"And now you know ours as well."

The joining of the Lightkeepers. The explosion of light. The howl of rage as the Dark Bearer had been forced out.

Darkness cannot exist in the light, Zach.

But it could put up a hell of a fight.

"How many of us were there that night," Zach asked. "A dozen?"

"More. Fourteen."

"Fourteen to overcome one? I suppose you've noticed those odds suck for us."

"They do, indeed. So, Zachary, now that you're a believer and you know the odds, are you with us?"

He held the professor's gaze. "I'm in. For now."

Professor Truebell smiled slightly. "Not quite the gung-ho response I'd hoped for, but it'll do for now. One last thing—" He folded his hands on the table and leaned toward Zach. "—I have to have your word. You'll do what you need to do, concerning Michaela?"

He hated this. She was his partner. Secrets put her in harm's way.

No, Zach. They make her safer.

He looked at Eli. *Get out of my head.*

You have to trust us.

I trust her.

"Zachary? Your answer."

"Yes. I'll tell her nothing of the Lightkeepers and nothing of the true nature of the events of that night."

"You won't regret it."

He regretted it already. "What's next?"

"We wait."

"For what?"

"The Dark Bearer's return."

Connect with the Authors Online:

Erica Spindler
Website: http://www.ericaspindler.com/
Facebook: https://www.facebook.com/EricaSpindler
Twitter: https://twitter.com/EricaSpindler
Instagram:
https://www.instagram.com/erica.spindler.author/

J.T. Ellison
Website: http://jtellison.com/
Facebook: https://www.facebook.com/JTEllison14/
Twitter: https://twitter.com/thrillerchick
Instagram: https://www.instagram.com/jt_thrillerchick/

Alex Kava
Website: http://www.alexkava.com/
Facebook: https://www.facebook.com/alexkava.books
Twitter: https://twitter.com/alexkava_author

J.T. ELLISONS BOOKS

STANDALONE THRILLERS
LIE TO ME (available September 5, 2017)
NO ONE KNOWS

A Brit in the FBI Series with Catherine Coulter
1 - THE FINAL CUT
2 - THE LOST KEY
3 - THE END GAME
4 -THE DEVIL'S TRIANGLE (available March 14, 2017)

Lieutenant Taylor Jackson Series
0 - FIELD OF GRAVES
1 - ALL THE PRETTY GIRLS
2 - 14
3 - JUDAS KISS
4 - THE COLD ROOM
5 - THE IMMORTALS
6 - SO CLOSE THE HAND OF DEATH
7- WHERE ALL THE DEAD LIE

Dr. Samantha Owens Series
1 - A DEEPER DARKNESS
2 - EDGE OF BLACK
3 - WHEN SHADOWS FALL
4 - WHAT LIES BEHIND

Available via Two Tales Press
THE FIRST DECADE: A Short Story Collection

Novellas with Erica Spindler and Alex Kava
(Featuring Taylor Jackson short stories)
SLICES OF NIGHT ("Blood Sugar Baby")
STORM SEASON ("Whiteout")

ALEX KAVAS'S BOOKS

THE RYDER CREED SERIES   **(In order)**
Breaking Creed
Silent Creed
Reckless Creed
Lost Creed (available Fall of 2017)

THE MAGGIE O'DELL SERIES   **(In order)**
A Perfect Evil
Split Second
The Soul Catcher
At The Stroke of Madness
A Necessary Evil
Exposed
Black Friday
Damaged
Hotwire
Fireproof
Stranded
Before Evil (available Summer 2017)

STANDALONE THRILLERS
One False Move
Whitewash

Original eBooks
A Breath of Hot Air (with Patricia A. Bremmer)

Novellas with Erica Spindler and J.T. Ellison
Slices of Night
Storm Season

Available via Prairie Wind Publishing
Off the Grid (A Maggie O'Dell Short Story Collection)

ERICA SPINDLER'S BOOKS

THE LIGHTKEEPER'S SERIES   **(In order)**
The Final Seven
Triple Six

STANDALONES
The First Wife
Justice for Sara
Wishing Moon
Fortune
Watch Me Die
Dead Run
Blood Vines
Bone Cold
Break Neck
Forbidden Fruit
In Silence
See Jane Die
Red
Last Known Victim
Copy Cat
Killer Takes All
Shocking Pink
Cause for Alarm
All Fall Down
Chances Are

Novellas with J.T. Ellison and Alex Kava
Slices of Night
Storm Season

A Note from the Publisher

First of all, I want to thank you for reading *SLICES OF NIGHT - a novella in 3 parts*. If you have enjoyed it I would be grateful if you would write a review. It doesn't have to be long—a few words would make a huge difference in helping readers discover new authors for the first time.

I also know that J.T., Alex, and Erica would love to hear from you. Please find them on all the social media sites and get in on the conversations on their personal websites. Currently they are working on future books for your enjoyment.

Keep reading!

Deb Carlin

Made in the USA
Lexington, KY
05 May 2017